SUMMER AT THE STABLES ON MUDDYPUDDLE LANE

Heart-warming, uplifting romance

Etti Summers

CHAPTER ONE

Rose Walker clapped with enthusiasm as her eight-year-old daughter Heidi guided her pony over jumps no higher than about a foot off the ground.

It might not appear to be a great deal to anyone else, but to Rose it was an achievement to be noted. Heidi had progressed from walking Parsnip over poles laid on the ground to actually jumping over said poles, all in the space of three lessons, and Rose watched and clapped as a succession of children popped the ponies they were riding over the same jump. All in all, there were nine children in the group riding lesson today. Heidi wasn't the youngest – little May

Halligan was, being only six years old –
but she was close to it, and although
Rose knew that children younger than her
daughter were able to jump far higher,
they were usually the ones who were
lucky enough to have their own ponies or
whose parents could afford more than
one lesson per week.

Horse riding wasn't the cheapest of
hobbies, but her daughter had been
horse-mad ever since Rose could
remember. The child seemed to have
been born with horses in her heart, and
she could clearly recall the first time the
not-yet-walking Heidi had seen a horse,
and the child's squeals of excitement,
followed by bereft sobbing as Rose had to
take her home, would be etched in her
mind forever.

After that, Rose had bought her a plush
pony toy to cuddle and a succession of
miniature plastic horses to play with. But
it wasn't enough. Heidi was adamant that

she wanted to firstly stroke a pony, then, once she'd achieved that goal, she wanted to get on its back. Her daughter's drive to learn to ride had been relentless, and it was Rose's one regret that she couldn't afford to buy the child her own pony.

Rose had resisted Heidi's pleas to have riding lessons for as long as humanly possible. But her daughter had been adamant and implacable. As she grew older, whenever Rose asked her what she wanted for Christmas or her birthday, the answer would be the same – a horse; or, if she couldn't have a horse, riding lessons. Rose had eventually given in, even though the cost made her wince, and from then on she'd had to sit in the viewing area of the indoor arena (which was a converted barn) no matter what the weather. Too hot in summer and absolutely freezing in winter, the experience wasn't a particularly comfortable one, and the hard plastic chairs put out for the parents to sit on didn't help either.

Heidi popped her pony over the tiny jump again and Rose called, 'Well done,' earning herself a disapproving look from Petra Kelly, who ran the stables. Petra was one of those people who preferred animals to humans, and Rose sometimes wondered if the woman actually preferred her horses to her farrier partner, Harry.

Heidi almost always rode Parsnip. Petra did her best to match rider with the horse or pony, and she liked to pair the two of them together for every lesson so they could get used to one another. Rose had begun to wonder which mount Heidi would be allocated when she outgrew Parsnip. Her daughter was almost there already, her legs a little bit too long for the animal, the proportions no longer quite as right as they had once been, and seeing the pair of them together reminded

Rose of a child outgrowing a bike and needing a slightly larger frame.

Heidi and Parsnip popped over the jump once again, relatively fluidly, although Petra scolded Heidi for allowing her elbows to stick out.

Heidi took the telling off good naturedly. If Rose had tried to tell her off like that, Heidi wouldn't have been quite so accepting. Sometimes her daughter could be as stubborn as the pony she was riding – he had a tendency to dig his heels in when he didn't want to do something.

'Oh, well done!' Rose cried, when little May Halligan, who was sitting on the back of a sweet Shetland pony, progressed from walking her mount over the poles on the ground to trotting over them. She watched the little girl rise into the trot, her cute face shining as she controlled an animal many times bigger than her.

Rose risked a quick glance at May's father, Jason. She didn't know much about him, apart from his name, and the rumour that he was a single dad. The woman who dropped May off at the stables for every lesson was the little girl's mum. She seemed pleasant enough, giving May a quick hug and a kiss before handing her over to Petra, who promptly handed the child over to one of the girls who helped teach the lessons.

For quite some time Rose had thought that Faith and Charity Jones were one and the same person, until she saw them side by side and realised they were twins. They kept their horses at the stables in exchange for helping out, and when Rose had learnt that, she had a vision of the future as she fully expected Heidi to suggest the same arrangement as long as Petra Kelly was in agreement.

Rose didn't want to think about that just yet; it was enough to bring Heidi to the stables once a week for an hour-long lesson, without having to ferry her daughter here every waking minute that she wasn't in school.

Finally the lesson was over and the children dismounted on their own and handed their ponies over to one of the adults, who shortened the stirrups then led any animals who wouldn't be used for the next lesson out of the arena.

Rose watched Heidi unbuckle her helmet and pull it off her head. Her blond ponytail was all askew, and strands of hair were falling around her face. Rose thought she looked adorable; but then she would, wouldn't she, because she was rather biased. It warmed her heart when Heidi, on noticing May struggling with her own buckle, went over to help the younger child.

Heidi was a good kid. Rose had never had a moment's trouble with her, and she could hardly complain about her obsession with all things equine. Not in the summer, anyway; however, the winter was a different matter.

Rose hated sitting there in the cold, bundled up and wearing practically everything she owned, shivering on the hard plastic seat while darkness descended rapidly outside and her breath steamed in front of her face.

No matter how many hot cups of coffee she drank from the vending machine in the corner, she invariably failed to keep herself warm.

Yet, on an afternoon like this, when it wouldn't get dark until about nine-thirty and the air inside the barn was warm and smelt of hay and horses (to her surprise she'd found she actually quite liked the smell of horse) it was much more pleasant. When she emerged from the indoor arena and she saw there was still a whole long evening of daylight ahead of her, she heaved a contented sigh.

The riding school was situated in rolling hills, with lush fields and hedgerows all around. The actual buildings themselves were constructed of old stone, which gleamed golden in the rays of the late afternoon sun. The drone of a tractor in the distance competed with the buzz of bees as Rose stepped outside to await her excited child. She smiled at the chickens scratching about in the yard, hunting for their supper, and she reminded herself to buy some of the eggs that Petra often had for sale. The yolks were so yellow they didn't look real, and the taste of them was far superior to anything she'd bought in a shop.

When Rose felt a small nudge on the back of her leg, she looked down to see Queenie, the stables' resident dog, staring up at her with large dark eyes.

'Hello sweetie,' she crooned, bending down to fondle her silky ears, and the spaniel wagged her tail. Rose actually enjoyed coming to the stables on evenings like this. Although Picklewick was hardly a metropolis, the village was a hive of activity compared to the peace and tranquillity which surrounded her here.

She'd just knelt down to tickle Queenie's tummy, the dog lying on her back with all four paws in the air and looking up at her hopefully, when the peace was shattered as Heidi dashed around the corner and skidded to a halt.

'Mum, Mum, you must come and see this!' She pulled at Rose's sleeve, and Rose clambered to her feet.

'Sorry, Queenie, maybe next week,' she said to the dog, who reluctantly rolled over onto her front and lay there looking at her reproachfully. 'What is it?' Rose asked her daughter. 'Don't tell me Petra has got another horse?'

Heidi very often demanded that her mum meet any new arrival at the stables, whether it was a new horse (which had only happened once), or some fluffy chicks that one of the hens had brooded.

'It's Tiddles, she's had babies! Come and see.' Heidi tugged at her again, and Rose allowed herself to be reluctantly dragged along. It wasn't that she was averse to seeing kittens – far from it – but she knew exactly where the conversation was going to go.

'Can we have one, Mum, please, can we?' Heidi pleaded.

Rose sighed. At least it was better than asking for a horse, she conceded, or a dog; they'd had that conversation, too. 'We'll see,' she said, which was her go-to comment when she meant "no" but she couldn't be bothered to argue.

Heidi whined, 'That means no.'

'Probably.'

They watched the kittens for a while, the cat giving her and Heidi a gimlet stare but not seeming to be unduly bothered by the attention, then Rose said, 'Come on, sweetie, we must get home. I don't know about you but I'm starving.'

'What are we having?'

Rose was just about to answer her when she heard a child's raised voice. Holding Heidi's hand, she came around the side of the building to head towards her car, and spotted May standing in the middle of the yard, her hands folded across her chest, her chin down, scowling up at her father from underneath her eyebrows.

'I'm sorry darling, but you can't. There isn't anyone to pick you up. I've got a meeting I can't get out of.' Jason caught Rose's eye and swiftly looked away.

'That's not fair!' May stamped her foot.

Rose tried not to look. It was difficult enough when your child had a tantrum, without having an audience to witness it. She unlocked the car and ushered Heidi inside.

'Why can't Mummy pick me up?' May demanded.

'You know Mummy has to work.'

'I hate you and I hate Mummy, too.' Another stamp, this time accompanied by a sob.

Rose opened the car boot, stowed Heidi's helmet in it, then fished out a pair of trainers and walked around to the passenger side to help her daughter off with her riding boots.

Jason Halligan knelt down so he was at eye level with his daughter, and said something to her that Rose didn't catch.

May let out a howl of despair. 'But that's ages away!' she cried.

Her dad said, 'It's two weeks, May, you'll only miss one lesson.'

'I don't want to miss **any** lessons. You promised you'd pick me up. Mummy said you'd always pick me up.'

Rose could see the conflict on the man's face, and she felt sorry for him. She knew what it was like when life got in the way of parenting.

Heidi wriggled out of her boots and slipped her feet into the trainers Rose held out for her. Rose walked around to the back of the car and popped the relatively clean riding boots inside, leaving Heidi to buckle herself into her seat belt.

'We could take her home with us, couldn't we, Mummy?' Heidi said.

Rose was about to get in the car, but her daughter's suggestion made her pause. She shouldn't interfere, but as they were here anyway, it made sense.

'Excuse me,' she called across to Jason Halligan. 'I'm sorry, I couldn't help overhearing; is your daughter going to miss her lesson next week?'

May's father straightened up. The look he gave her was an assessing one, and Rose wasn't sure she liked it.

'That's right,' he said, his tone clearly indicating it was none of her business.

She was about to turn away and leave him to it, when she caught sight of May's little face. It was streaked with dirty tears, and her bottom lip was wobbling. Her heart went out to the child, so she tried again.

'I could bring her home with Heidi, and you can pick her up from my house, if you like. We're going to be here anyway, so it won't be any trouble,' she added just in case he thought it might be.

'Thank you, but no. I'm sorry, May,' he said, turning to his daughter. 'You're just going to have to miss next week.'

'It's not fair,' May cried, shooting her father daggers. 'Why **can't** Heidi's mummy bring me home?'

'Because I won't be finished until late, that's why.' He sent Rose an apologetic look.

Rose smiled back. At least this was better than the annoyed glance he'd given her earlier. She followed her smile up with a nod, saying, 'That's okay, I don't mind having her until you're ready to pick her up.'

'No, sorry, May. I've made my decision.'

'See,' the little girl said defiantly. 'Heidi's mum doesn't mind. It's you who minds. You don't want me to go riding.'

'That's not true,' her father protested, but May cut in with, 'Yes, it is. I heard you tell Mummy.'

'Okay, I do mind, but only because I worry about you.'

Rose thought she'd better beat a hasty retreat before she caused any more trouble. She got in her car, snapped on her seat belt and started the engine, hissing when she put her hands on the steering wheel. She must remember to face the car the other way and not leave it in the full glare of the sun. She'd forgotten how hot the interior could get, so she wound the window down to try to get some air.

She was about to pull off, when she saw Jason Halligan's exasperated expression. May was having a right tantrum and Rose bit her lip. Oh, dear, this was her fault; if Rose hadn't offered, then maybe he would have talked May around by now.

Feeling guilty, she called through the open window. 'It honestly won't be any trouble to pick her up from riding. In fact, I could collect her from school along with Heidi, and bring them both to the stables. And how about I give her tea afterwards? I'm sure she'd like that.' The damage was already done, so Rose might as well try to make amends.

The effect on May was instantaneous. The little girl stopped crying and clapped her hands together. 'Daddy, can I? Please say yes. Please?'

Jason Halligan narrowed his eyes at Rose, but she guessed he didn't want to come across as the bad guy, because he reluctantly agreed. 'If you're sure?' he asked, clearly hoping she wasn't.

'I'm sure,' Rose hastily reassured him. 'I often fetch other people's children from school and feed them, and they do the same for me when I can't pick Heidi up. It's no trouble, honestly.'

'You'd better give me your address and phone number,' Jason said.

Rose switched off the engine, clambered out of the car and they duly swapped phone numbers, Rose adding her address. 'Don't forget to let May's teacher know I'm picking her up,' she reminded him. 'They're very strict about who collects the children, and I wouldn't want May to be stuck in school while someone is trying to get hold of you.'

'Right, okay. I'll see you next week,' he said, before adding a totally reluctant, 'Thank you.'

As Rose drove away she glanced in the rear view mirror to see May hopping up and down excitedly. She was pleased she'd made the little girl's day a bit better, but she felt awfully guilty for interfering. What went on between May and her father wasn't any of her business, and she'd had no right to step in but, as she'd told him, it was second nature to help out other mums, and they helped her out in return.

She couldn't see any harm in it, so why had Jason Halligan seemed dead set against the idea?

Jason Halligan had no intention of taking Heidi's mother up on her offer. Agreeing to it had just seemed to be the easiest thing to do at the time; he didn't think she was going to take no for an answer, and May was having such a tantrum he was starting to get embarrassed. He would have agreed to anything in order to stem his daughter's tears.

He'd give it a day or two, then have a chat with May and explain. With a bit of time and distance, he was sure she'd understand.

In a way, a little part of him was relieved that she wouldn't be going riding next week. He had never liked the idea of Pamela dropping her off at the stables and the child being unsupervised until he arrived after he'd finished work. But unless he picked her up from school himself, which he wasn't able to do, he didn't seem to have any choice in the matter. Pamela and May had sorted the riding lessons out between them, and had only informed him when it was a fait accompli. Usually he managed to arrive not long after the lesson started, so there were only a few minutes when his daughter was left to her own devices, but he still hated it. Petra Kelly and the girls who helped out with the lessons were marvellous, but May wasn't their responsibility. She was his – and

Pamela's, although you wouldn't always know it.

Another reason he didn't like May taking riding lessons was the danger. The Shetland pony she rode might be small in horsey terms, but he was still massively bigger than she was. When Pamela had told him May was having riding lessons, he had been horrified. He still was. Many years ago, when he was a child himself, he remembered a boy in his class whose mum had been a keen rider. He also remembered the devastation on the face of the boy when he'd come into school one day after a period of being absent, and learnt that the boy's mother had suffered an accident whilst riding. She'd broken a bone in her neck and had been paralysed from the neck down. Jason wondered what had happened to her – and the boy, because shortly afterwards the kid had been removed from the school and Jason had never seen him again.

Logically, Jason knew that the odds of something so terrible happening to May were slight. But he'd made the mistake of researching riding accidents on the internet, and it had made him even more reluctant to allow May anywhere near a horse.

He wondered if other parents felt the same. Was it normal to feel such worry that your child might be thrown? How did other mums and dads cope? He supposed it might be easier for the parents of those children who had grown up around horses, or even if he'd had some experience of the animals himself. But the closest he'd got to anything resembling a horse, was a donkey ride on the beach at Weston-Super-Mare when he was little. And that had been before the boy's mother had been injured. Since then, he'd made a point of avoiding the large, hairy beasts; until, that is, May and her mother had conspired against him to let her have riding lessons, and now he seemed to be

in a perpetual state of mild panic
whenever she was at the stables.

Take today for instance; his heart had
been in his mouth when May had guided
the pony over the poles laid on the
ground. Walking hadn't seemed too bad,
but trotting the animal over them had
appeared reckless. And Heidi's mother,
Rose Walker, hadn't seemed in the least
bit concerned when her daughter took a
proper jump for the first time. Admittedly,
the pole was only about a foot high, but it
still meant that for a brief moment all
four of the horse's hooves were off the
ground at the same time. It wouldn't be
long before May progressed to that stage,
and he didn't think his nerves could stand
it.

'Daddy, Daddy, Daddy!' May squealed, as
he tried to get her into the bath. He
always insisted she had a bath every
evening, and never more so than when

she'd been riding, because afterwards she always smelt vaguely of horse.

'I can't wait for next week!' she cried, and his heart constricted. She'd talked about nothing else since he'd bundled her into the car at the stables and driven home. 'I like Heidi,' she said, 'even though she's a bigger girl than me.'

That was another problem – how much older was Heidi than May? 'What year is Heidi in?' he asked.

'I'm in year two and she's in year four,' May said proudly. 'She's eight and I'm six, and she's invited me for tea.'

Technically it hadn't been Heidi who had done the inviting, it had been her mother. Jason wasn't sure how he felt about that. As far as he knew, May hadn't had a play-date after school before, although he knew she'd had one or two during the school holidays because Pamela had told him. He left that kind of thing up to her.

After a day at work, the last thing he wanted was to entertain someone else's child. He simply wanted to be on his own with May, so the thought of her going to someone else's house for a few hours and impacting on his precious time with her didn't please him.

It was bad enough when work necessitated May having to go to her grandma's, which was what should have happened next Thursday if he hadn't stupidly given in to letting a total stranger pick her up from school and take her to her lesson. Not only that, the total stranger would be taking his daughter home from that lesson too, and May would have to stay there until he fetched her. This was a woman he'd never met before. Okay, he conceded, he **had** met her before, but he'd never actually spoken to her. The only thing he knew about her was that she had a daughter, Heidi, who was older than May and in year four in school. That was it.

It was hardly a substantial basis on which to allow the woman to take care of his child.

'I like Heidi,' May was saying. 'She's kind. Did you see she helped me take my helmet off, Daddy? I couldn't undo the buckle thing.'

That was true; usually one of the twins who helped with the lessons unfastened the helmet for her. It wouldn't be long before she could do it herself, he thought, with a pang. She was growing up so fast – far too fast for his liking. It seemed only last year she was a tiny babe in arms, and now here she was getting all excited about play dates.

'I can't wait to tell Mummy tomorrow,' she continued, piling bubbles on her head and wetting hair that he'd had no intention of washing this evening.

'May!' he scolded, but his admonishment was tinged with laughter. She looked so silly and incredibly cute with her pink face, wet eyelashes and a bubbly head.

She threw a handful of bubbles at him and giggled at his pretend shocked expression.

Hoping that was the end of the going-to-Heidi's-house conversation, he lifted her warm slippery body out of the bath and wrapped her in an oversized fluffy towel.

No such luck.

As he was dressing her, she said, 'I like Heidi's Mummy. She hasn't got a daddy.' May held onto his shoulder to steady herself as she put one foot into her pyjama bottoms, then the other.

'Rose Walker hasn't got a daddy?' Jason asked, confused.

'No, silly. **Heidi** hasn't got a daddy. Not the way I've got a daddy.'

'Not many mummies and daddies share their children, like me and your mummy do.' This wouldn't be the first time he'd explained their arrangement to her.

'Why not?'

'Because it's usually the mummy who takes care of the children most of the time, and the daddies don't see their children as often as I see you.' He pulled her pyjama top over her head.

'They must be so sad. You'd be sad if you didn't see me every day, wouldn't you?' This last came out rather muffled, then her head popped free of the neck of her pyjama top.

'I would be very sad indeed,' he admitted.

'Do you think Heidi's daddy is sad?'

'I don't know, poppet. I don't know anything about him.'

'I think he is. I think Heidi is sad, too.'

Abruptly, Jason wondered if Rose Walker's offer to pick May up from school was more for Heidi's benefit than to enable May to have her riding lesson. Was Rose trying to fill her daughter's time with friends because Heidi's father wasn't on the scene?

It was entirely possible, and he realised how lucky May was, despite the inconvenience that living between two households caused. He might dislike the arrangement, but it was the best thing for May. Of course, the ultimate best thing for her would be to have both her parents living under the same roof, but that simply wasn't going to happen.

He wished he could blame his ex-wife for their relationship failing, but it hadn't been anyone's fault. Falling out of love had crept up on them both without either of them realising it, and by the time they had, it was too late – the love had well and truly disappeared. Yet they might have carried on living together for May's sake, but Pamela had fallen in love with a builder called Craig and that, as they say, was that.

'I'll cheer her up, won't I, Daddy?' May said.

'You, my lovely girl, are enough to cheer anyone up.'

'I wonder what we'll have for tea?' she mused. 'I hope it's fish fingers.'

For a second Jason was confused – they'd already had their tea. Bath was a prelude to bed, so why was she talking about—? Ah, she meant what she was going to have for tea when she went to Heidi's house.

He was about to try to change the subject, in the hope that if he didn't respond she would eventually forget about her visit to Heidi's next week, but when he looked at her eager little face, he knew he had to take the bull by the horns. May wouldn't forget, and she was looking forward to it so much. He hated to be the one to play bad cop, but it was for her own good and—

She was still looking at him, but her expression now held a hint of worry. 'You **are** going to let me go, aren't you, Daddy? You **said** you would.'

Indeed he had, but at the time he'd felt coerced into it by his daughter and by Rose Walker. 'We'll see,' he said, and watched as May's bottom lip began to tremble.

Wonderful. He should have put his foot down from the start and not given in to pressure. Now he was going to upset her right before bedtime and it would be ages before he would manage to settle her down.

Jason spied the bottle of wine sitting all alone in the wine rack and turned away. As much as he fancied drowning his sorrows, he couldn't. One glass might well lead to two, or maybe more, and having to get up in the middle of the night to see to a fractious child when he'd had a bit too much to drink was never a good idea. Besides, he had work in the morning, and he had to drive May to her mum's house first.

Instead of the wine, he flipped the switch on the kettle and made himself a cup of tea, taking it into the living room and sinking down onto the sofa.

May had an incredible knack of making him feel like the worst father in the world. She'd certainly done so tonight, and, he conceded, she might have a point. First he'd said yes, and he'd built her hopes up, and then he'd said no and had dashed them to smithereens.

He knew she didn't mean it when she'd told him she hated him – all kids said that to their parents at some point, although usually it was when they hit their teenage years, and not at the tender age of six. But May had been through a lot in her little life; despite how much he and Pamela had tried to shield their daughter from the breakup of their marriage, it was inevitable she would be affected.

What the hell was he supposed to do about next week? He knew if he asked Pamela for advice, she wouldn't see the harm in allowing Rose Walker to pick May up from school, take her riding and then take their daughter to her house for some tea.

But his issue was that he didn't know anything about Rose Walker, or her home life. All he knew was that he'd seen her at the school gates occasionally, chatting to other mums, and she and Heidi seemed to adore each other. Was that a good enough reason to allow the woman to look after his daughter?

Throughout the whole separation and divorce, his mother had been the voice of reason. No matter that the divorce had been amicable and inevitable, there had still been a great deal of heartache surrounding his and Pamela's separation, and even more hurt when Pamela had moved in with her new partner. Craig seemed a nice enough bloke, but that was another thing Jason didn't like very much, the fact that May spent nearly fifty per cent of her time in another man's home.

He knew he was a bit of a helicopter parent, but he couldn't help it, even though he had a feeling he was being somewhat over-protective. Maybe he should give his mum a call – her advice was always sage.

After he'd explained the problem, Sheila surprised him. 'I don't know why on earth you're fussing,' his mother said. 'Unless you have reason to suspect this woman won't take good care of May?'

He didn't. 'No...'

'Well then, you've got nothing to worry about. You've got to let go of the reins sometime, you know. May is growing up; you can't keep her wrapped in cotton wool forever.'

But that's exactly what he wanted to do. Ever since his divorce, he'd felt very acutely that she was his sole responsibility, even though he shared joint custody with Pamela. When May was in his care he wanted to make sure he did everything he could to keep her safe.

'You've got to let her spread her wings a little,' his mother added. 'That's the problem with parents today – they don't allow their children to learn to stand on their own two feet and develop some resilience.'

'You've been on one of those training sessions again,' Jason said.

'What if I have? It doesn't make what I'm telling you any less true.'

Jason shrugged, despite his mother not being able to see him. She worked as a learning support assistant in what May called "the big school". His daughter was referring to the secondary school she would eventually go to when she was eleven. He didn't want to think that far ahead.

'What are you afraid of?' Sheila asked.

Crikey, where should he start? For himself, he wasn't scared of anything. When it came to May he lived in a permanent state of anxiety, from the worry of whether he was feeding her enough vegetables, to the very real fear of what would become of her if something was to happen to him.

No one told you that being a parent meant you were faced with a lifetime of worry, and he knew it would only get worse as she grew older. He actually dreaded the thought of her learning to drive—

'Are you going to let her go or are you going to stifle her for the rest of her life?' Sheila demanded, breaking into his thoughts.

'Excuse me?' He was flabbergasted at the stance his mother was taking. For some reason, he'd expected her to agree with him. That she'd taken the opposite position, shocked him somewhat.

'You heard,' Sheila said. 'Let Rose Walker look after May for the afternoon; what harm can it do?'

What harm indeed?

CHAPTER TWO

Rose grimaced as her mobile pinged again with yet another text from May's father asking if May was okay. May was as fine as she had been the last time he'd messaged, which had only been fifteen minutes ago. If Rose had known Jason Halligan was going to be this needy, she would never have offered to pick his daughter up from school and take her riding.

However, when she looked at May and Heidi trotting around the arena, both of them rising and falling in their saddles with effortless ease, her expression softened. The girls were having a wonderful time, and that's what mattered.

Rose left it ten minutes before replying and when she did she also sent him a photo of his daughter smiling so widely that it almost brought tears to her eyes. The child was having the time of her life and had been ever since Rose had picked her up from school, popped both girls home so they could change into their riding clothes, before driving them out to the stables on Muddypuddle Lane.

Heidi and May had chattered and giggled the whole time, talking non-stop about their school friends, their teachers, and their love of anything remotely horsey. Rose was proud of the way Heidi was taking May under her wing, and she could see how May was looking up to Heidi and hanging onto her every word. It was quite sweet to see them together; they could almost be sisters, despite their appearances being very different. Heidi followed Rose in that she had fine blond hair and grey eyes. May's hair fell down her back in dark, glossy ringlets, and she had hazel eyes. With her cute button nose and slight frame, she reminded Rose of a porcelain doll, despite the golden tan she'd already acquired this early in the summer.

Rose had re-plaited May's hair for her as it had come free at some point during the day, and had helped her secure her helmet, checking it was tight enough but not too tight, before she sent both girls scampering off into the arena to await the arrival of their ponies.

Taking her usual seat, Rose had proceeded to answer the third text Jason had sent her (the first had been to ask if she'd picked May up from school, the second had been to ask if they were on their way to the stables, and the third had been to ask whether they'd arrived) and then she had settled down to watch the lesson. It had only just started when Jason had sent her a fourth text, which she'd just replied to.

She wondered how long it would be before he sent her the next. Considering he was supposed to be working, Jason seemed to have plenty of time to send her messages.

She looked up from her phone in surprise as someone took the seat next to her.

It was one of the mums Rose knew from school, Jane Crease. She seemed nice enough, and they'd exchanged a few pleasantries now and again, but they weren't that friendly and Rose wondered what she wanted.

'Did I see little May Halligan getting out of your car?' Jane asked.

Ah, so that's what Jane was after, a bit of gossip. 'Yes, you did.'

'Getting friendly with her dad, are you?'

Jane certainly knew how to cut to the chase.

'Not at all,' Rose replied coolly. 'I offered to bring May to her lesson, otherwise she would have missed it.'

'Bit of an odd setup, isn't it?'

'I don't think me offering to bring May to her riding lesson is that odd.' Rose was busy trying to work out what could possibly be wrong with it.

'Not that; him and his ex-wife.'

Despite not wanting to gossip, Rose couldn't help asking, 'What do you mean?'

'May lives with both of them. Co-parenting, it's called. I think it should be called confusing. I bet the poor little mite doesn't know whether she's coming or going most of the time. She spends the week with him, and the weekends with her. The poor thing is being bounced back and forth between the two of them like a ping pong ball.' Jane seemed to take great delight in telling Rose this.

'May seems happy enough to me,' Rose said. 'Whatever they're doing, it appears to work.'

Jane gave her a shrewd look. 'Kids need stability,' she said firmly, as though she was an authority on the subject.

'Kids need love,' Rose countered. 'And it seems to me that May is loved very much.' Rose had the text messages to prove it.

'It's like that, is it?'

'What's like what?'

'He's rather good looking,' Jane said.

'Who? Jason Halligan? I hadn't noticed.' It was a lie, because it was hard **not** to notice. Not many people wouldn't. But just because she thought someone was good looking, didn't mean to say she had the hots for them, which was what Jane was implying.

Jane snorted, clearly not believing her, and when the woman got up to return to her original seat, Rose realised their brief chat had been a fishing expedition. She guessed news of her bringing May to the stables would be all around the school yard by tomorrow. How ridiculous. It looked like you couldn't do anyone a favour these days, without someone taking it the wrong way.

Rose sat through the rest of the lesson wondering if Jane and the other mums were talking about her, and she was pleased when it finally ended.

Making her way outside, she hoped for a quick getaway, but she'd not taken into account a new notice on the board outside the office, as Heidi and May came haring up to her, all legs and excited faces, and dragged her to take a look.

'Petra says we need to sign up by next week,' Heidi cried, jumping up and down with excitement.

'What are you talking about?' Rose couldn't help laughing at the earnest expressions on both girls' faces.

'The gymkhana! Petra told everyone about it at the end of the lesson. Weren't you listening?'

That will teach her to dash off like she did – she'd missed a vital announcement. She peered at the piece of paper pinned to the board.

'Mum...?'

'Shhh, I'm trying to read it.'

'What's a gymkhana, Mrs Walker?' May asked.

'Oh, it's a bit like your sports day, only with horses. There'll be games and competitions.'

'What kind?' May's eyes were as large as the hooves belonging to the pony she'd just ridden.

'I don't know.'

'Do you think there'll be show jumping?'

'Maybe.'

'What about dressage?' Heidi asked.

'You'll have to check with Petra. I've not really got any idea.' She didn't think there had been dressage at last year's' gymkhana, but she couldn't remember.

'Can you put my name down, Mum?'

Rose fished a pen out of her bag and wrote Heidi's name on the sheet of paper. Then she noticed May's hopeful little face.

'Sorry, sweetie, I can't put your name down – your daddy will have to do that.'

'Mum,' Heidi said, 'Please put her name down – it might get full up. Her dad can cross it off next week if she's not allowed.' She waggled her eyebrows to let Rose know she understood that May's dad probably **would** cross his daughter's name off, but she didn't want May to realise, and Rose's heart swelled with love.

She was so lucky to have such a mature and considerate child.

'Okay, I will, but if her dad is cross, I'm blaming you,' Rose warned her with a smile.

Names written, she hastily rounded the two girls up, ushered them into the car and headed for home.

As she drove, the children chattering in the back, her thoughts strayed to May's father. She hadn't given much thought about the little girl's home life, but now Jane had mentioned it, Rose couldn't help considering it. Jane seemed to imply that the child was pushed from pillar to post on a regular basis, but May seemed happy and well adjusted.

The temper tantrum she'd thrown at the stables last week was perfectly normal; Heidi had thrown far worse in her time, and from what other people had said, it was nothing compared to the teenage angst that was to come. Whatever was going on between May's parents didn't seem to have affected the little girl too badly.

Rose's phone pinged with an incoming text and she shook her head wryly, guessing the latest message would be from Jason inquiring how the lesson had gone and whether May had got through it safely.

He'd have to wait; there was no way she was going to even look at her phone let alone answer a message while she was driving. Anyway, he'd texted her enough times already, and she was getting fed up. The man really needed to loosen the apron strings a bit.

One thing occurred to her though, as she made her way through the village, and that was how she was surprised he allowed his daughter to go riding at all. He seemed extremely over-protective, yet he happily allowed May to bounce up and down astride a creature many times larger than she was. It was quite irritating to think Jason Halligan trusted a Shetland pony more than he trusted her.

Oh, well, she said to herself, there was nowt so strange as folk, as the old saying went. She was pretty sure she wouldn't be helping him out again, despite how sweet May was.

Rose simply didn't need the aggro.

Jason checked his phone for possibly the hundredth time, and sighed when he realised Rose Walker hadn't responded to his latest text. What was she **doing**? It was less than fifteen minutes since the riding lesson ended, so she must still be at the stables. Surely she could take a second or two to send him a quick reply, before she drove the children home?

If he'd been regretting allowing Rose to take May to her riding lesson before, he was doubly regretting it now. He'd been on edge since this morning, first worrying about whether Rose would actually remember to pick May up, then fretting about whether she'd make sure May's helmet was firmly on (even though he knew the staff at the stables would double-check anyway) and that was in addition to his normal worry that May might fall off her pony, or one of the unpredictable creatures might kick her, or bite her, or knock her over. He even had a moment where he was concerned that the cockerel, who for some reason was called Fred, might decide to peck her.

And now that the lesson was over with, he had fresh worry regarding the drive home from the stables to Rose Walker's house, followed by whether the two girls would get on, and accompanied by concerns over what the woman would feed his child for tea.

It was now over twenty minutes since the lesson had officially ended and there was still no word from Rose. No wonder he was going grey. Every now and again he scrutinised himself in the bathroom mirror looking for new grey hairs, his heart sinking every time he found another. At the rate he was going, he'd be totally grey by the time he was forty. No wonder people resorted to dyeing their hair. It had crossed his mind more than once. He was only thirty-six, yet he was starting to look ancient, and he very definitely felt it. No one ever told you that kids would age you so much. But even if they had, he wouldn't swap May and his grey hairs for the absence of worry and a dark barnet.

His phone vibrated and he snatched it up. Finally!

When he read Rose's message he was surprised to see they were already at her house. Gosh, it took him at least twenty minutes to wrestle May away from the stables. She absolutely adored it there and loved every animal, from the smallest of chicks to that massive ex-racehorse which Petra rode. She insisted on saying hello to as many of them as she could, but her favourite was Gerald the donkey, although she had a soft spot for the goat as well.

Jason didn't. Why a creature with eyes like the devil was called Princess he had absolutely no idea. It didn't help that the animal had once tried to eat his sleeve.

He replaced his phone on the table, and tried to concentrate on the conference call he was supposed to be involved in. He didn't like working this late, but his company had clients in the US and it was barely midday for them. The Americans were so gung-ho it made his teeth ache.

He loved his job, he really did, but it wasn't the be-all and end-all. May was that, and he resented anyone and anything that took him away from her. It wasn't so bad during the day because she was at school, but as soon as school was out, he wanted to be too. He was more than happy to work from home once she had gone to bed, but right now he was becoming increasingly more resentful as the minutes ticked on, that someone else was spending time with his daughter instead of him.

He wondered what she was doing now. Was she behaving herself? Of course she was – she always did, apart from occasionally when she was with him. He preferred it that way; being polite and respectful at school and with other people, but allowing herself to have the odd meltdown when she was at home.

He hoped Heidi Walker wasn't teaching her anything he would disapprove of. Or that her mother was allowing them to watch something inappropriate. Or that—

Give it a rest, he told himself; Heidi seemed a perfectly lovely child. Rose seemed a perfectly lovely woman. The children were probably watching a Disney movie, or playing dress-up or something. But he still couldn't help worrying.

He sighed, then was brought firmly back to the present when his boss said, 'Is there anything you would like to contribute, Jason?'

Jason tried not to panic. He had absolutely no idea what they'd been talking about for the past few minutes. Or since the meeting had started, if he was honest. He shook his head. 'No, I think you've covered everything,' he said.

His boss nodded, and Jason let out a small sigh of relief. It looked like he'd got away with it this time. He'd better concentrate from now on, though, he thought.

But less than two minutes after the meeting had ended he was in his car and heading to Picklewick. If he was lucky, he might get there before Rose fed the girls, so he could take May home and enjoy eating his evening meal with his daughter.

Rose was just about to dish up three platefuls of risotto with some spicy chicken (mildly spiced, to cater for younger palates) and roasted vegetables, when there was a knock at the door.

With a cross sigh she went to answer it, wondering who it could possibly be. She was getting slightly fed up with all the interruptions to her afternoon. Thankfully, she'd not had a text off Jason for a while so she assumed he was actually doing what he was paid to do, rather than fretting about his daughter.

How she managed to resist the urge to roll her eyes when she opened the door and saw May's father standing on the other side of it, was a miracle. Dear god, she felt sorry for the poor child, having a father like him. If he was like this now, Rose could only imagine what he would be like when May started going out and about on her own; he'd be horrific. He'd be even worse when May had her first boyfriend. Although, the way Jason was going, May might very well be in her thirties before that happened.

'I didn't expect you so soon,' Rose told him, the irritation evident in her voice.

'My meeting finished a bit earlier than I anticipated,' he said, 'So if it's all right with you, I'll just grab May and we'll be off.'

'Actually, I was just dishing up,' she replied mildly, hiding her annoyance. He could at least let them eat before he took May.

'Oh, we won't bother you for much longer,' Jason said, looking past her into the depths of the house.

Rose invited him in, although she wasn't sure whether she wanted to, but she could hardly keep him out when his daughter was inside. 'She's upstairs, playing with Heidi. I'll give her a shout.' She halted at the foot of the stairs. 'May? Can you come down please, your father is here.'

There was an abrupt silence, then two pairs of heavy footsteps stampeded across the landing, and two heads peered around the bannister.

May did not look pleased to see her father. In fact, she looked positively thunderous.

'Daddy, why are you here?' she demanded.

'To take you home.' Jason smiled up at his daughter who, Rose noticed, failed to smile back.

'You're early. I haven't had tea yet,' May said.

'I know; isn't that lovely? We can eat at our house.'

'I don't want to.' There was a thud, and Rose realised May was stamping her foot. She seemed to do that a lot.

'We can't intrude on these lovely people any longer. It's time we went home.'

'No, Daddy, it's not. Heidi's mummy said she would give me tea, and I haven't had my tea yet, so I'm not going home and you can't make me.'

Rose bit her lip, hoping no one would see her smile. May was a right little madam and a bit of a handful, but she knew what she wanted and Rose could only admire that.

'I could do pancakes...?' Jason said.

'No, thank you. Heidi's mummy is making roasted vegetables. I want those.'

Jason shot Rose an incredulous look. 'Vegetables?'

Rose nodded. 'Cooked in the oven, with some oil and garlic.'

'May has agreed to eat it?'

'Yes, why? She's not allergic to garlic or anything, is she?'

'No, I think it's the vegetables she's allergic to.'

'We're having risotto too, and a little bit of spicy chicken.'

Jason raised his eyebrows. 'Risotto **and** spicy chicken?'

'Yes, you're welcome to stay and eat with us, if you like. There's plenty to go round. I always make far too much and end up having to eat it myself, as you can tell.' Rose cringed as his eyes swept up and down her body. Why on earth had she said such a thing?

'We couldn't possibly—' Jason began, but his daughter had other ideas.

'Yes, we can, Daddy. You said I could stay for tea. If you take me home I'm not eating any of your yucky food.'

'But you like my cooking,' he said.

'Not today I don't. Today I want Mrs Walker's cooking. I've never had roasted vegetables, or spicy chicken.'

'That's because you don't like vegetables very much. I have to hide them in your food to get you to eat them.'

May stared at him suspiciously, and Rose simply knew the child was filing this little bit of information away to use against him in the future. She had a suspicion May would be scrutinising every single meal Jason put in front of her from now on, to try to find hidden vegetables.

'If you don't want to stay and eat with us,' Rose said to him, 'you could always come back in an hour. I must get on though, otherwise everything will be ruined.' She walked into the kitchen, leaving him standing at the bottom of the stairs. He was starting to get on her nerves.

'May, please calm down. It's time to go home,' Rose heard him say, and she also heard his daughter's very firm, 'No! You **promised.**'

Rose quickly put a spoonful of risotto on each plate, and as she was doing so she became aware of someone standing behind her.

She turned, spoon poised. 'Are you sure you don't want to stay?'

'I suppose I'm going to have to, if I want my daughter to eat anything this evening.'

Right. Good.' She was having difficulty keeping a lid on her temper. What an ungrateful man. 'You can make yourself useful and lay the table,' she said, jerking her head at the drawer where the cutlery was kept. 'Is there anything you don't like – how about vegetables?'

'I like vegetables just fine,' he said. 'I just wish May did, too.'

'They all seem to go through these funny fads,' Rose said, doing her best to be pleasant. 'Heidi went through a phase of not wanting anything red on her plate. Considering she loved tomatoes, it was a bit of an issue. I remember her sitting at the table once, bawling her eyes out because she wanted blue tomatoes, not red.'

She heard him clattering about in the draw as he chuckled, 'That's funny.'

'Glad you think so. I certainly didn't at the time. She seems to have grown out of that now, although I'm sure there will be another along shortly. You think you've got over one little hurdle, and along comes another. Thankfully, it doesn't matter in the great scheme of things,' she added, 'but it can be annoying at the time.'

She used oven gloves to put the warm plates on the table, then indicated he should sit down. 'Yours is the one with the biggest portion,' she said to him. 'I'll just give the girls a shout.'

Rose took a second to compose herself as she walked out of the kitchen towards the stairs. Since he'd made the decision to stay and eat with them, he'd mellowed slightly, and she found she liked him all the better for it.

'Heidi, May, your food is on the table. Can you wash your hands first, please?'

A flurry of small footsteps followed her call, then Rose heard the tap running. She was about to walk away, when May's voice floated down the stairs. 'Has he gone yet?'

'No, your father is going to have tea with us.'

'Oh.' May didn't sound pleased about it. 'Do you think he'll let me play afterwards?'

'I don't know, sweetie, you'll have to ask him.'

'Tell him if he's good he can have some wine,' May said, appearing at the top of the stairs with a towel in her hand. Rose saw Heidi's arm reach out to take it from her. Then both children hurtled down the steps, coming to a halt at the bottom.

'He likes wine a lot,' May said in a loud whisper. 'Tell him he can have some if he lets me stay. Do you have any?'

'I do, although I don't think I'm going to get a bottle of wine out right now,' Rose told her, stifling a laugh. She wasn't quite sure whether May was telling her that her father was a lush or not, and she didn't want to find out. She also didn't want him to think she made a habit of swigging back glasses of wine when she was looking after other peoples' children. Although technically, now he was here, she wasn't looking after May. May was now her father's responsibility, but she still didn't want Jason to get the wrong idea about her. Rose had a bottle or two of wine in the house, but she didn't drink often; she actually didn't like the taste very much, and neither did she like the effect when she was drinking it, or the hangover the day after.

'I think you should,' May persisted as Rose rounded up the two children and ushered them into the kitchen.

'What do you think she should do, May?' Jason asked.

'Never mind,' Rose said quickly. She'd assumed this conversation was just between her and May, but May proved her wrong.

'I told her she should give you some wine if you say I could stay after we've eaten our tea,' May said. 'Can I stay for a bit? Please? Heidi said she'll show me how to draw horses.'

This time Rose was unable to hold her laughter in when she saw Jason's stricken expression. He looked utterly mortified and totally embarrassed.

'You can't have any secrets when you've got children,' Rose said.

'It's not a secret,' Jason said, then he added hastily, 'Not that I make a habit of telling everyone how much wine I drink. I don't actually drink much. Just the odd glass now and again.' He was clearly flustered, not wanting her to think the worst of him.

'My vice is chocolate,' Rose confessed. 'Although I only tend to eat it when Heidi is in bed.'

'Mum! You eat chocolate when I'm in **bed**? Why don't I get any?'

'Because it rots your teeth and it's not good for you.'

Heidi pointed out, 'You're old but your teeth aren't rotten.' She turned to May and said, 'Did you know that old people have to have all their teeth out and they have to have plastic ones.'

May's eyes grew round. 'Really?'

'That's not true at all,' Rose said. 'Some people have problems with their teeth, and yes some people do have to have all their teeth removed, but not everyone.'

Heidi put a hand up to her mouth and whispered behind it, 'My great-grandma keeps her teeth in a glass in the bathroom. It's yucky.'

'She keeps plastic teeth in her bathroom?' May asked in fascination.

'I've seen them.'

Rose sent Jason an apologetic look. 'It's true, my grandma does keep her false teeth in the bathroom. Thank god dental hygiene is better today, eh?' Then she giggled. 'I can't believe we're having a discussion about false teeth and dental hygiene.'

She was pleased to see Jason tucking into his meal with enthusiasm, and so were the two girls. Whether May did, or didn't, like roasted vegetables seemed to be neither here nor there, because the chatter around the table was distracting the child enough for her to continue putting forkfuls into her mouth until her plate was empty.

Jason didn't say anything but she could see him looking, and when Rose got to her feet to collect the plates he said, 'You've eaten a good meal, May.'

'That's because it was nice,' the child said, and once again Rose burst out laughing.

'Are you trying to say your dad can't cook?' she asked.

'No, my mummy can't. She's not as good at cooking as Daddy is, and Daddy's not as good at cooking as you are.'

Rose took the compliment. These days she didn't get many, so she wasn't picky where they came from. 'Thank you, young lady,' she said. 'You may come again.' As soon as the words left her mouth, Rose wished she could take them back. She gave Jason an apologetic look, but to her surprise, he didn't seem annoyed.

'Can I stay for a little bit, Daddy? Please?'

'Only if it's all right with Rose. And Heidi, of course.'

Heidi nodded. 'Come on.' She grabbed May's hand and they made a dash for the door.

After the girls left, Rose said, 'Ordinarily, I would insist Heidi helps with the clearing up, but not when she's got guests.'

'Does she do many chores?'

'Not many, just one or two. I don't want her to grow up thinking she has an inbuilt maid. I expect her to put her dishes in the dishwasher and to keep her room tidy. I also expect her to take her school bag upstairs, empty it out, and then give me anything I need to wash, or read, or sign. I don't think it's too much to ask.'

'May doesn't do anything,' he said, and she could see him thinking. 'When did you start?'

'House-training Heidi? From when she was quite small. We used to make a game out of picking her toys up and putting them away before she had her tea.'

'I usually do all the clearing up and tidying up after May has gone to bed.'

'Do you mind me asking you something?' Rose thought he was definitely going to mind, so she added, 'You don't have to say anything if you don't want.'

'Go on.' His voice was cautious, and she thought he was going to tell her to mind her own business.

'You and May's mum don't live together, do you?'

'No, we don't.'

'Does she live with you?'

'She lives with us both,' he said, and he went on to confirm what Jane had told her earlier, finishing up with, 'It's not ideal by any stretch of the imagination, but at least it means she gets to see an equal amount of us both, which she wouldn't do if she lived with one or the other of us.'

'I'm not judging', Rose said, anxious in case he thought she was. 'If it works for you, that's all that matters. Families come in all shapes and sizes these days, and at least May gets to see both of you equally.'

'Does Heidi see much of her father?'

'Not a great deal. Holidays and the occasional weekend, and her birthday – that's about it. I'm lucky my dad is so hands-on with her. She adores her grandad, and she gets some male input into her life.'

'Thank you for picking May up from school and everything,' he said when there was a lull in the conversation. 'I'm sorry I texted you so often. It's just...I worry about her.'

'Don't we all!' Rose exclaimed. 'I think that's par for the course when you have kids. You get handed a whole lot of worry from the minute you conceive and according to my mum, it doesn't end when they enter adulthood, either. She still worries about me as though I'm twelve.'

'I know what you mean; my mother worries about me, too.'

He was helping stack the dishwasher, as if working in her kitchen was the most natural thing in the world, and she was surprised he'd gone from being so tense, to being fairly relaxed. He was actually quite easy to talk to, now that he'd got over his constant worry about May. With his daughter safely playing upstairs and a decent meal eaten, he seemed more chilled.

'Would you like a coffee or a tea?' she asked. 'I don't think the girls are quite ready to end the evening yet.'

He checked the clock on the kitchen wall. 'It's still quite early,' he said, 'although I do want her to be in bed by seven-thirty.'

'Heidi goes to bed at eight, nine o'clock on a Friday or Saturday. To be honest,' Rose added, 'some days I'd be quite happy if she went to bed at half-past seven, too.'

'I have evenings like that,' Jason admitted. 'I love my daughter and I enjoy her company, but crikey, I sometimes think I'm too old for this.'

'How old are you?' Rose wanted to know.

'I'm thirty-seven.'

'That's hardly old, is it?'

They continued to chat back and forth for another half an hour or so, until Jason finally decided it was time to leave. Rose called to the children, smiling when disappointed groans wafted down the stairs, although May was willing enough to collect her things together, with a little help from Heidi.

'Thank you for having me, Mrs Walker,' May sing-songed to Rose and Rose ruffled her hair.

'You're welcome, sweetie. We'll see you at the stables next week, yes?'

May nodded vigorously, then she gasped and slapped a hand to her forehead. 'I just remembered! Daddy, Daddy, there's going to be a gymkhana at the stables and Mrs Walker put mine and Heidi's names down for it.'

Jason looked baffled. 'A what?'

'A gymkhana – think school sports day with ponies,' Rose explained for the second time that day.

'When is this?'

'A month away, so there'll be plenty of time for the children to practice.'

'I'm going to do show jumping,' May announced grandly, not noticing the horrified look on her father's face or the hardening of his jaw.

'I don't think so,' he replied sharply.

'But, Daddy—'

'Hurry up, May, we need to go home. I'm sure Rose has other things to do. Thank you for having her. Us.'

'You're welcome,' she said as Jason hurried his daughter out of the door and into his car.

'Bye, Heidi, bye Mrs Walker,' May called and Rose grimaced – the little girl seemed cheerful enough now, but she guessed it wouldn't last long when her father informed her that she wasn't going to be entering the gymkhana.

Rose felt somewhat guilty about putting May's name down and maybe she should have asked Jason first, but she hadn't seriously imagined he wouldn't allow May to enter. It was the highlight of the riding year (apart from the nativity play) and every child wanted to enter it. May would be devastated.

'May's dad is a bit grumpy, isn't he, Mum?' Heidi said.

Downright rude would be a more accurate description. Why on earth she'd thought he was nice earlier, was beyond her. Nice wasn't a word she associated with Jason Halligan.

Attractive was a word that popped into her mind, but no matter how good-looking he was, she preferred friendliness over sexy any day. And Jason didn't appear to have any of that whatsoever.

That was the last time she'd do him a favour, although it was a pity Heidi and

May wouldn't see each other again apart from during their riding lessons and at school. The children seemed to get on exceptionally well – but the adults most certainly did not.

CHAPTER THREE

Jason had been in two minds about whether to take May to her riding lesson the following week. His daughter had been fractious and difficult ever since they'd driven home from Rose and Heidi's house and he'd informed May that she wasn't, under any circumstances, going to take part in any competition involving a horse.

He'd tried telling her she wasn't old enough, but she'd insisted she was, and she'd even managed to get her mother on board. The only thing in Jason's favour, he saw, as he walked into the office to pay for May's lesson and spotted the notice, was that the gymkhana was being held on the third Saturday in June, and that was the date on which Pamela and Craig would be away for a long weekend so Jason was looking after May. If he hadn't been, then it would have been inevitable Pamela would take May to the event.

He and his ex-wife needed to have a serious conversation about singing off the same hymn sheet when it came to their daughter, because right now they were poles apart regarding May and her riding.

Jason saw Rose before she saw him, and he was tempted to wait for May out in the car park because he didn't want to speak to the woman. He couldn't believe she'd put May's name down for the competition without his permission. What a cheek! It had caused no end of problems between him and his daughter – and between him and his ex-wife, who couldn't see how potentially dangerous riding could be. It was bad enough having May dashing around an indoor arena once a week – but he knew that as she grew older and became more confident, she wouldn't be content to merely do circuits of a barn. She'd want to ride outside, and the first step on that slippery slope was the gymkhana.

His heart sank when he caught a glimpse of what his daughter was doing, and he decided he had to stay to see what was going on.

Petra had placed five poles several metres apart along the length of the arena, with the riders and their ponies gathered at the one end. May was guiding her pony between the poles as though she was performing a slalom, weaving in and out as fast as she could to the cheers and whoops of the rest of the riders and the parents in the raised spectator area.

May was about to wind her pony around the final pole and Jason found himself urging her on.

'Go, May!' he shouted and beamed with pride as she cleared the last pole, hauled her pony around it and hurtled back towards Petra and the others. The **hurtling** was more of a fast trot rather than a breakneck gallop, but his daughter seemed to be flying, closing the distance with heart-stopping speed.

Petra blew a whistle when May and her pony trotted over a line drawn in the sandy floor, and everyone cheered and clapped, Jason along with the rest. He'd moved closer to the balustrade without realising and was now standing near Rose, who'd leapt to her feet and was clapping enthusiastically.

'Didn't she do well?' Rose exclaimed, turning to him, her face alight.

Jason found himself nodding. Then he calmed down and asked, 'What exactly are they doing?' Because he had no idea what was going on.

'Practising for the gymkhana.'

'But May's not entering the gymkhana,' he protested. 'I thought this was supposed to be a riding lesson.'

'It is. These events all help with a rider's control of their mount, as well as being fun.'

'She's still not going.' He was adamant about that – and he wasn't pleased they were practising for it, either.

'That's your decision, of course,' she said, but Jason was sure he could hear an undertone of disapproval in her tone.

How dare she question his parenting? It was his job to keep May safe, and he believed by preventing her from entering a reckless and pointless competition he was doing precisely that. Thank god he only had to see Rose once a week, because she was starting to get on his nerves. It didn't matter that he'd enjoyed eating a meal with her, but she'd overstepped the mark by signing May up for this darned event and now he was certain she was silently commenting on the way he was bringing his daughter up.

'Yes, it is,' he replied coolly, then stalked outside to await his child. He knew May would be upset that he was missing the remainder of her lesson, but she'd get over it. It was more important that he had as little to do with Rose Walker as possible right now.

He'd reckoned without May, though, because the first thing she said when she emerged through the large doors to the arena was, 'Me and Heidi are having a play date.'

'Really?'

May nodded emphatically. 'Grandma says one good turn deserves another. It means you have to do something nice for someone if they do something nice for you.'

'I know what it means.' He tried to hurry her away, but May was having none of it.

'Can I tell Heidi she can come for tea today?' she persisted.

'No, you can't.'

'Could she come tomorrow?'

'I'm sorry, poppet, but I don't think that's a good idea.'

May pouted. 'You never let me have any friends over. You're mean.'

'I'm not mean. It's just...' How do you explain to a six-year-old that you don't want her bothering with another child because you don't approve of the child's mother; especially since there was nothing intrinsically wrong with the woman. If he was honest, Rose was actually quite nice – pretty, friendly, helpful, pretty (that was twice in the same thought he'd referred to her as pretty). She was also interfering and judgemental, but he couldn't tell May that; she wouldn't understand, and she also might repeat it.

'You don't want me to have any friends.' May was taking her argument to the next level.

'Of course I want you to have friends.'

'But you don't want me to be friends with Heidi.'

Darn it, his daughter was far too perceptive for her own good.

'You can't stop me being friends with her.' May gave him a sly look. 'I'm friends with her in school, so there.'

'That's fine,' he replied absently, taking her hand and trying to hurry her to the car.

She pulled her hand from his. 'If I can be friends with her in school, why can't I be friends with her when I'm not in school?'

She had him there, and he didn't have an answer – at least, not one he was prepared to share with her. He was already the bad guy in her eyes; he didn't want to make things worse.

'Because I said so.' His reply was vague and didn't make a great deal of sense, which pained him, because he always tried to be honest with his daughter.

'That's not a good enough answer,' she told him, and he was shocked at the sudden maturity in her voice.

'It's the only answer you're going to get, young lady,' he said.

'Don't you like Heidi?' May asked, as he opened the car door and lifted her inside.

'Yes, I do.' He eased his daughter's riding boots off and reached into the back seat for her trainers.

'Do you like Heidi's mummy?'

He hesitated, and that was all it took. May pounced on him. 'Why don't you like Mrs Walker? She's nice. She's pretty, too. Not as pretty as Mummy, though.' She sneaked a look at him from under her lashes.

'No one is as pretty as your mummy,' he said to her, kissing her on the top of her head.

'But, do you think Mrs Walker is pretty, too?'

He'd been thinking that very thing not too long ago. 'Yes, she's pretty. Now—'

'Mrs Walker!' May yelled. 'My Daddy thinks you're pretty.'

'May!' He couldn't believe she'd just said that. He turned around and saw Rose getting into the car next to his. She was looking amused and he felt a blush creep up his neck.

'She asked me whether I thought you were,' he said in his defence.

'I think he likes you,' May continued, and Jason slowly closed his eyes. This couldn't be happening.

He opened them again, glared at his daughter and hissed, 'Stop it!'

May stared innocently back at him. 'What?' she asked. 'You said I always had to tell the truth.'

Grr. Just wait until he got her home, he'd— Actually, what **would** he do? He could hardly chastise her for telling the truth, something he always encouraged her to do.

'What day did you have in mind?' Rose asked. 'May didn't say.'

'Excuse me?'

'To come to yours? The play date? Tea?'

Jason didn't know what to do with himself. Out of the corner of his mouth he said to May, 'Did you already tell Heidi she could come to tea, and did you invite Rose, too?'

'Uh huh.' She nodded. Oh, dear.

His shock must have shown on his face because Rose hastily said, 'You didn't know about it, did you?'

What could he say? His daughter had already landed him in enough trouble and caused him enough embarrassment, without this.

There was only one thing he **could** do.

'Of course I did,' he said plastering a smile on his face and hoping it would stay there. 'We were just discussing which day was best, weren't we, May?' He nudged her foot with his knee.

'Daddy said you can come tomorrow, didn't you, Daddy?'

'Yes, that's right, tomorrow. If that's okay with you?' He hoped May didn't see the fingers he'd crossed behind his back – with any luck Rose would have something else on.

'Um...okay. Tomorrow is good. We weren't doing anything.' Rose smiled hesitantly at him.

'Yippee!' May clapped her hands together and kicked her feet, catching him on the shin.

'I'll text you our address,' he said to Rose. 'Will five o'clock do you?'

'Lovely. We'll see you then. Bye, May.'

'Bye, Mrs Walker.'

'I think if your dad and I are going to be friends, you should call me Rose,' she said.

And all the way home Jason had to listen to May say "Rose this" and "Rose that", until he was sick of hearing the woman's name.

But when he'd put his exhausted daughter to bed he discovered he was still hearing Rose's name in his mind long after May had stopped saying it.

Rose kept herself together until she was in the car, then she couldn't help bursting out laughing.

'What's so funny, Mum?' Heidi asked.

'May's dad,' Rose replied. 'I swear to god he had no idea May had asked us to pop over for tea one evening. Did you see his face?'

'He looked like a bulldog chewing a wasp,' Heidi said with a giggle.

'Where on earth did you get that expression?'

'Nana.'

Rose shook her head. The things her daughter came out with.

'May's dad still isn't happy with us, is he?'

'No, I don't think he is. Did May say anything to you about being allowed to enter the gymkhana?'

Heidi shrugged. 'A bit. She said he's being mean and that her mum said she could enter.'

'I wonder why her mum isn't taking her to it?' Rose mused. 'I thought she lived with Jason during the week and with her mum on the weekend.'

Heidi reached for one of the wipes that was kept in the glove compartment, and cleaned her hands. She then stuffed the used wipe into the side pocket of the car door.

'Heidi, I hope you remember to bring that out with you. I don't need my car filling up with rubbish.' Out of the corner of her eye she saw Heidi pull a face. It wouldn't be long before her daughter was in full teenager mode, and Rose was dreading it.

'May's dad is looking after her when the gymkhana is on,' Heidi told her. 'May said her mum and her stepdad had to go somewhere.'

'That's unfortunate. I got the impression that although he didn't like her riding, her mum didn't mind.'

'That's what May said. You don't mind **me** riding do you mum?'

Rose didn't, because she'd ridden herself when she was a girl, but it was only since she'd become a parent that she realised how much her mum used to worry about her being on the back of a horse. It wasn't so bad riding in the arena, but Rose used to go out for hacks over the hills with her friends. The stables they frequented were quite happy to let the youngsters loose on their own.

It would be unheard of today, and Petra would never dream of letting anyone take her ponies out without supervision, but things had been different when Rose was young. Rose could see where Jason was coming from, even though she thought he was too over-protective.

'I don't **mind**,' Rose said, 'but I do worry.'

'You always worry about everything.'

'It comes with the territory. It's my job to worry.'

Another roll of the eyes from Heidi was followed by a huff.

Rose thought it wise not to say anything further regarding Jason and May. Bringing up May was Jason's business, not hers, and it must be hard for him only having his little girl half of the time. She knew how much she worried whenever Heidi's dad looked after her. It wasn't that she didn't trust Ben – she knew he loved Heidi as much as she did – but she couldn't help it. So she felt a certain degree of empathy for Jason.

She also felt a certain degree of something else, too, and that was attraction. It went against the grain a bit, because he was a grumpy so-and-so and she could do without grumpy people in her life. But on the other hand, she'd seen another side of Jason Halligan when he had eaten an evening meal with them last week. It had been a friendlier, more relaxed Jason; a Jason she found she quite liked.

The problem was he'd reverted to the Jason she had originally met the second May had told him about the gymkhana.

One part of him was Rhett Butler and the other part was more Ashley Wilkes, and she didn't know which one she preferred. The one was moody and enigmatic, and the other was friendly and far more open. The problem was she quite liked them both, and to put them into one package, aka Jason Halligan, was quite a dangerous combination.

Thank goodness she was no Scarlett O'Hara.

CHAPTER FOUR

Rose wondered whether she should take something to Jason's house. She'd spotted May's mum at the school gates picking her daughter up this afternoon, and she wondered if she should say anything. Or whether May would. She gave the little girl a quick wave, then turned away hastily, feeling awkward.

If she took something, would it seem more like a date? Because it quite clearly wasn't – the only date was the play date between the two children, and the fact that May had invited Rose along too, even though her father knew nothing about it. He'd rallied well though, she conceded.

Maybe she should take a bottle of wine? On the other hand, maybe not. Taking wine was more like the sort of thing you would do if you were going to a dinner party. Besides, she wasn't sure it would go very well with chicken nuggets. Although, she may be doing him a disservice by assuming that was the sort of thing their meal would consist of; she had no idea how good a cook he was, and she might be in for a surprise.

Perhaps she could take dessert? But then again, would he think she was being patronising? Or that he'd think she didn't believe him capable of providing dessert? Oh, dear, this wasn't easy. If any of Heidi's other friends' mums had invited her, she knew exactly what she'd do – she'd take cake. That seemed to be the done thing. Not that she'd been invited to anyone's house for tea very often; it was normally a mid-morning or mid-afternoon thing, when cake was entirely appropriate.

Perhaps it was best if she took nothing at all, just herself and her daughter?

Decision made, she supervised Heidi getting changed out of her school uniform and into something more appropriate, before she went off to check her own appearance. Jeans, tee shirt with a cardi slung over the top, and a pair of ballet flats. It was her usual attire, but for some reason she felt she should make more of an effort. But if she made more of an effort, wouldn't that look a bit odd? She was only going to his house for a bite to eat while the two children played: it was hardly an evening out on the tiles.

She had a sudden image of being in a bar sipping cocktails with Jason Halligan, and her eyes widened. Where on earth had that come from? Although she wasn't closed to offers of evenings out from the opposite sex – she'd done her fair share of dating since she'd split from Heidi's father – she wasn't exactly in desperate need of a man. She and Heidi were a unit, and they were quite content together.

For the moment.

Rose was under no illusion that as Heidi got older, she'd want to spend less and less time with her mother. Which would leave said mother at a bit of a loose end. Rose didn't want to rush out and fill the void which Heidi's growing independence would inevitably leave, but neither did she want to become a lonely old maid.

Therefore, she wasn't averse to dating.

But what she was averse to, was imagining she was going on a date with Jason.

Things were too complicated there, even if she **was** interested in him. Which she wasn't. Not really. And he wasn't interested in her, either. She ignored the memory of May telling her that Jason found her attractive. **Pretty** was the word the little girl had used. Jason hadn't been delighted either, but then again, he'd been so embarrassed he probably couldn't even remember what his name was. The poor man – that's what kids did to you. When they were younger they caused you inordinate amounts of embarrassment. Rose was looking forward to doing exactly the same to Heidi when Heidi was old enough. There had to be some compensations, and that was one of them.

Rose checked her appearance in the mirror, deciding she'd have to do. She would have liked to put a swipe of gloss on her lips, but she didn't want Jason to think she'd been making an effort, especially since lip gloss wasn't the sort of thing she normally wore.

'Ready?' she called, and Heidi came bounding down the stairs. Her daughter appeared to be ready for anything. She too was dressed in jeans, but that was where any sign of normality ended. She was wearing wellies on her feet, despite it being summer and there hadn't been a drop of rain for ages, and she had pink glittery angel wings on her back and a swimming cap on her head. Not only that, she'd draped a woollen scarf around her neck.

'That's an interesting outfit,' Rose said mildly.

'I'm not sure what we're going to be doing, so I thought I'd dress for any eventuality.'

Rose shook her head in bemusement. It was a constant source of wonder hearing what came out of her daughter's mouth. She had no idea where the **any eventuality** phrase had come from (although she strongly suspected Heidi's granddad was the culprit), but she couldn't fault the child's logic. Even though she guessed that neither the wellies, the scarf, nor the swimming cap would actually be needed today.

'Could you find my car keys for me, please?' Rose asked. 'I just need to nip to the loo.'

It was a diversionary tactic; she knew exactly where her car keys were and she didn't need the loo. What she needed to do was to stuff a pair of Heidi's trainers and a fleece into her bag, just in case the children played out in the garden and the wellies hindered Heidi from running around.

She was glad she had, because on arriving at Jason and May's house May immediately dragged Heidi outside. 'I've got a trampoline,' she declared and Rose heard the little girl ask, 'Heidi, why are you wearing Wellington boots?'

'I was wondering the same thing,' Jason said as he showed Rose into the kitchen.

'I've no idea. Her fashion choices are a mystery to me. I'm sure there must be some logical explanation, but I have no idea what it is.'

'Is that a...?' He tapped his head.

'A swimming cap? Yes, it is. I've no idea about that, either. Or the scarf.'

'I do like the fairy wings, though,' Jason said, and they both burst out laughing.

This might be easier than she'd anticipated, Rose thought, as he switched the kettle on. She perched on the stool at the breakfast bar and watched him getting some mugs out of the cupboard and pop a tea bag in each. He was quite a bit taller than her, broad shouldered and slim hipped. Not too brawny but not too skinny either. Just how she liked a man. Not that she liked this one – well, she did, but only in the sense that she could admire a decent looking guy without wanting to jump into bed with him.

A blush whooshed up her face. Dear god, did she just think that? She had a sudden image of crisp white sheets and a dark-haired head on her pillow.

Mortified, she pushed it away. This wasn't the time or the place to be having fantasies.

There was an awkward silence and she wondered what to say to fill it. The most logical thing to talk about would be the stables. It was one of the things she and Jason had in common, but it would be fraught with pitfalls if his reaction to May entering the gymkhana was any indication.

'What do you do?' she asked, her brain gratefully latching onto the subject of work. 'For a living, I mean.'

He poured boiling water into the mugs, added some milk and gave them a quick stir before handing one of them to her. 'I work in renewable energies,' he said. 'Behind a desk mostly. What about you?'

'I'm an administrator, so I work behind a desk, too. I'm part-time though, so I only work during school hours.'

'Do you like your job?'

'I do, actually. I work in the care home out on Albany Road. Do you enjoy yours?'

'Yes, I do. I feel as though I'm doing my bit for the planet.' He got a pot out of a cupboard. 'I'm making chilli with rice, if that's okay with you?'

'With hidden vegetables?'

He laughed. 'How did you guess? Shredded carrots are my speciality. May will eat them if they're covered in chilli sauce. She picks out the red kidney beans, though. It's a very mild chilli,' he warned. 'May isn't too keen on spicy.'

Rose wondered if that was strictly true. May seemed to have had no trouble eating the spicy chicken that she prepared last week. The little girl's tastes might very well be changing and Jason might be slow to catch on. It had happened with her and Heidi. In fact, that was the only thing Rose could be sure of with Heidi, that things were in a constant state of change. What might be her daughter's favourite one day, would be looked upon with scorn and derision the next. Rose had learnt to play things by ear and go with the flow.

They drank their tea, then Jason began preparing their meal.

 'Is there anything I can do?' she offered.

'Thank you, but no. I've got it all sorted.'

She glanced around the kitchen, wondering whether his ex-wife had had any hand in its decoration. It looked quite functional, but then again it was a kitchen. She hadn't seen the living room and she wondered if there were any throws and cushions. What was it with men and their general dislike of cushions?

Why on earth was she thinking about soft furnishings when she had Jason Halligan standing in front of her, his hips moving slightly as he stirred some mince in a pan.

Those hips were quite delectable. As were his shoulders and his broad back. He was wearing a tee shirt, and she could see the muscles flex in his upper arm and a smattering of hairs on his forearms. He had nice hands, too. Wait, **what**? What on earth was she doing? Anyone would think she fancied him.

Okay, to be honest she did, a bit. But she must stop this. He was the father of her daughter's friend and that's all there was to it. She really needed to go out on another date; it might stop her fantasising about Jason. Although, if her last couple of dates were anything to go by, she might be fantasising about him even more after she'd been on another disastrous one.

Hunting around for a safe topic to talk about, Rose found she was struggling. He didn't want to talk about the stables, and they'd already touched on both their home lives. When he came round to hers last week they had talked about school and teachers. They didn't have much more in common, as far as she could tell.

'When you aren't working or looking after May, what do you do with your time?' she asked, eventually.

'The usual – I read, I do housework, I catch up on my sleep.'

'Your life sounds about as much fun as mine,' Rose joked, then bit her lip. 'Sorry, I didn't mean it to come out like that.'

'No, you're right; what with working all week and looking after May, by the time the weekend comes I'm bushed.' Then it was his turn to bite his lip as he turned to her. 'Sorry, that was a bit insensitive of me considering I do get the weekends to myself and you probably don't.'

'Not much,' she agreed. 'Ben lives too far away to see Heidi very often, but that's okay, I cope. My mother is as good as gold, and she will look after Heidi if I ask.'

There was a clatter at the door, and two small heads peered into the kitchen.

'When's tea ready, Daddy?' May asked.

'About fifteen minutes. Why don't you wash your hands, and you can show Heidi your bedroom. I'll give you a shout as soon as the food is on the table.'

Rose watched them go, May holding Heidi's hand and tugging her through the kitchen. 'She's a credit to you,' she said. 'She's absolutely adorable.'

'She's an absolute madam,' Jason said. 'Look what she did to me last—' He stopped abruptly, and his eyes skittered away from hers.

Rose laughed. 'Don't worry, I know what you were going to say, and that's fine. I'd already guessed that May had railroaded you into inviting us around for a meal.'

'I'm sorry, it wasn't like that.'

'What **was** it like?' Rose wasn't being awkward, she genuinely wanted to know. 'Was it because of the gymkhana?'

'Yes, partly.'

'What was the other part?' Rose felt was holding something back, and she hoped he wasn't going to say he had a girlfriend.

He wiped his hands on a cloth and turned to face her, leaning against the worktop. 'I didn't want it to come across as anything it wasn't,' he said. 'Please don't take that the wrong way.'

'How am I supposed to take it?' Rose was bemused. It wasn't as though they'd been flirting or she'd been coming on to him, so where he'd got this notion from she had no idea.

'It's just I've got to be careful around May,' he said.

'Are you talking about dating? Because if you are, I don't think this is a date.'

Jason frowned and looked at his feet. 'I'm sorry, I'm not expressing myself very well, am I?'

'No, you're not, but I know what you mean. Since Heidi's father and I split, I haven't dated much, and I wouldn't want to introduce another man into Heidi's life until I was absolutely sure it was serious. So far, that hasn't happened yet. There's no need to worry on that score; I'll treat you the same as I treat any other parent of Heidi's friends. Just because you're a man and I'm a woman, doesn't mean our children can't enjoy each other's company.'

There, it was out in the open. It looked like he'd been having similar thoughts as she, but now neither of them needed to worry. All that mattered was that the children were happily playing together, and she and Jason could have a friendly conversation, without either of them worrying that the other thought it meant more than it did.

Strangely, though, it wasn't relief coursing through her, but disappointment. Oh well, it was better this way. The last thing she wanted was to date the father of Heidi's new best friend, and then for her and Jason to fall out for some reason. It would just make things very awkward and very difficult.

This was for the best, wasn't it?

Jason wasn't sure he'd handled the conversation very well. In fact, he wasn't quite sure exactly what he'd said. And neither could he read Rose's reaction. He had the feeling he'd just told her he wasn't interested in her. He wasn't interested in any woman, but something inside him said he was fibbing to himself. He **was** interested in Rose. She was pretty and fun, quite sparky, but in a nice way, not in the way Pamela had been towards the end of their marriage when they seriously hadn't liked one another at all.

But whether he was interested in Rose or not, made absolutely no difference. He wasn't in the market for a girlfriend and he was pretty sure she didn't like him in that way. Which made him feel a bit of a prat, considering what he'd just said to her. She'd made it clear that all she wanted from him was friendship because of their daughters, and for no other reason. On the odd occasion when he picked May up from the school gates (that was normally Pamela's job, then she'd drop May off at his house as she was on the way to work) he'd noticed Rose was always surrounded by other mums, quite happily laughing and chatting in a group. He wasn't kidding himself that she was only interested in being mates because she didn't have anyone else. She appeared to have loads of friends.

May also had plenty of friends in school, and he was well aware Pamela occasionally had those friends around to play, and May sometimes went to theirs. But during the week, when he had May in the evening and overnight, he never encouraged her to go anywhere or to have anyone back to his house. Heidi Walker was the first child, apart from May, to walk through his front door, and Rose Walker was the first woman who wasn't related to him.

He knew he was being selfish in wanting to keep May all to himself, but it wasn't doing her any good. He was aware enough to wonder if some of his antipathy to his daughter having riding lessons was because it impinged on his precious time with her, and not solely because of the hazards. He was also aware enough to know that this precious time would soon be gone. Before he knew it, his daughter would be a teenager and he'd be lucky if he got a grunted hello out of her.

Of course, not all teenagers were like that, and he didn't have any experience of them, but from what his brother, who had two teenage boys, had told him, he was fully expecting it.

He turned his attention to rinsing the rice in boiling water, but as he did so he felt a totally unexpected and unaccustomed pang of loneliness. When he came to think of it, it was quite sad that the only real friend he had was Rose Walker, whom he hardly knew at all and who was only friends with him because of their daughters.

So it was in the spirit of friendship that he found himself asking, 'Do you fancy going out for a meal sometime? Just the two of us?'

And he was pretty sure that Rose, after her initial blink of surprise and slightly shocked expression, had said she would love to because she was only being friendly.

So why was his heart thudding at the thought of being on his own with her, without the children?

CHAPTER FIVE

'I feel like a kid truanting from school,' Jason said, and Rose laughed as they stepped inside the pub.

She knew exactly what he meant because she felt the same way herself. It was so rare for her to go out at all, and when she did it was normally with Heidi in tow, or going somewhere where Heidi wanted to go.

'Who's looking after May? Is it your ex-wife?' Rose asked.

'Pamela? Yes, she always has her on the weekend. How about you? Who's babysitting Heidi?'

'My mum. Heidi is sleeping at her house tonight.' Rose wished she hadn't said that. It sounded as though she was telling him the way was open for him to come back to hers for some after-dinner fun.

No doubt it **would** be fun, but it so wasn't going to happen, and she didn't want to give him the impression it would. He wasn't interested in her in that way, despite him asking her out to dinner, (she had the feeling he was lonely) but even if he **was** interested, there was no way she was jumping into bed with him on the first date.

But this wasn't a date, so that was irrelevant. This was just two friends having dinner, wasn't it? And she didn't have any option other than to treat it as though it was, although she did feel a little awkward being out with him. That was mainly because she fancied the pants off him, especially considering he looked delectable in a pair of jeans and a shirt which had the top two buttons undone. He was the epitome of smart-casual, whereas she felt slightly overdressed in a playsuit which she'd bought last year to go on holidays and hadn't worn since, so she thought it was about time it had an airing. She'd felt quite smart and sexy in it whilst standing in front of her bedroom mirror, but now that she was sitting opposite him in a little gastro-pub in the middle of nowhere, she actually felt rather immature wearing it. It was the sort of thing much younger women wore, not mothers in their mid-thirties.

'Have you been here before?' she asked and soon they were discussing food choices, their likes and dislikes, and the places where they had eaten out in the past. Then they moved onto box sets and films, before talking about music. And in between they chatted about the girls, and school, their jobs, and their families, until Rose felt she had got to know him considerably better. He was actually easy to talk to and he seemed genuinely interested in her, unlike some of the other dates she'd been on in the dim and distant past where her companions had only wanted to talk about themselves; which, according to some of her single friends, was quite normal.

Jason, on the other hand, seemed to take a genuine interest, asking her questions and listening to her answers. Once or twice she wondered whether it was a diversionary tactic to avoid having to talk about himself, but whenever she asked him a question he seemed more than happy to reply.

Rose popped to the loo after dessert and before coffee, and while she was reapplying her lip gloss, she quickly checked her phone. Heidi had sent her a goodnight text and had followed it up by saying,

Hope you're having a lovely time. Grandma says she hopes you're behaving yourself.

At least, that's what Rose thought it said, as she tried to decipher Heidi's spelling.

Rose sighed. 'Thanks, Grandma,' she muttered under her breath, knowing Heidi would probably ask her what Grandma had meant by that comment.

For one brief moment, as she slipped back into her seat and caught Jason's eye, she wished she wasn't going to behave herself – but that was silly. Anyway, she wasn't going to have any choice, more's the pity.

Hang on a second, she was back to thinking about him like that again, and it simply wouldn't do. But how could she help it when she was sitting across the table from one of the best looking men she'd seen in a long time, and one who seemed to have eyes only for her?

This just wouldn't do, Jason was thinking to himself as he watched Rose walk across the restaurant and re-join him at the table. She looked gorgeous in the all-in-one thing she was wearing; he wasn't sure what it was, but it suited her. She looked lively and full of fun, and young and vibrant, and he could see other men's eyes following her progress across the room and the swift envious glances of the women as she passed.

She was very attractive, and as she picked up her coffee and pursed her lips to take a sip, a thought flashed into his mind – what would it be like to kiss her?

Well now, he said to himself, back off fella. This wasn't a date, and he hadn't asked her out; this was just a couple of friends sharing a meal without the kids.

Oh, for Pete's sake, who was he kidding? He knew when he'd asked her that it hadn't been out of friendship, no matter what he'd said to himself at the time. He'd wanted to spend some time with her alone without the girls.

And if she hadn't been so adamant that she just wanted to be friends, he would have considered this a date.

He hastily looked away, not wanting her to see how attracted he was to her. She didn't need to know; it would do neither of them any good. But when she licked a little bit of froth from her upper lip, his eyes focused on her mouth and he couldn't seem to drag his gaze away.

'What?' she asked. 'Have I got a foam moustache?'

'No, you're good.' He swallowed convulsively, thinking she was more than good, she was gorgeous.

As he continued to look at her, he saw the faint blush on her cheeks and his heart constricted. What on earth was she doing to him?

It must be because he hadn't been out with a member of the opposite sex since the last time he and Pamela had gone out for a meal, he told himself. The novelty was clearly going to his head. Anyone would think he didn't know how to behave around an attractive woman, but he felt gauche and awkward compared to her confident and easy manner.

Before he could say or do anything further to embarrass himself, he signalled to the waiter for the bill.

He saw Rose reach for her purse, and said, 'Let me get this. I asked you out.'

'Okay, but only if you let me pay for the next meal.' Her eyes widened as she realised what she'd said, and he wondered whether she was regretting coming out with him. 'I mean, if there is a next time,' she stuttered. 'If you'd like there to be. I'd like to have another meal out with you, if you would. Oh, dear.'

He stared at her. 'Can I ask you something? Have you ever been riding?'

Rose stared back at him, then she eventually said, 'Pardon?'

Damn it – did she think he had been about to suggest going out again? Twit, of course that's what she was anticipating, considering they'd only just been talking about it. And then he went and asked a ridiculous question like that.

'Riding, have you ever been?' he repeated, feeling a right plonker.

'Um, yes, I used to ride quite a bit when I was younger.'

'Why did you stop?'

'Boys, pubs, too expensive...' She laughed self-consciously.

'Did you ever fall off?'

'Of course I fell off. Everyone who rides falls off at some point.'

'Were you ever scared?'

'No. Never. Excited and exhilarated, but never scared.'

'Did it hurt?'

'Falling off?' She shrugged. 'Sometimes; it depends. Once I fell off because I forgot to do the girth up and the whole saddle slipped. I landed on my bum. The only thing I hurt that time was my pride. The ridiculous thing was the horse hadn't even taken a step. I broke my leg once, though. That hurt a lot.'

Jason felt a shard of ice jab him in the stomach. The thought of May being injured made his blood run cold. 'How did it happen?'

She gazed at him steadily, for far longer than the question warranted. 'I fell down the stairs at home.'

Jason's mouth dropped open and he closed it again hurriedly. 'It wasn't anything to do with horses?'

'No. I know you want to minimise any kind of risk to May, all parents want to do that, but there's even risk in your own home. I was injured more in my house than I ever was when I was out riding.'

'I can see what you're trying to do,' he said.

'I'm not trying to do anything. I'm just pointing out that bubble-wrapping kids doesn't work. May has found something she loves doing – for now. Like I did, she might very well grow out of it. In fact, she probably will. And yes, riding can be dangerous. But so can gymnastics, skiing, ice hockey, rugby...' She stopped.

Jason got her point. He'd played rugby himself in the past, and if May had been a boy he probably would have actively encouraged his son to play. But maybe not at six years old.

'Those horses are so big compared to her,' he said.

'Yes, but what she's doing at the moment is as safe as riding gets. Tango is a gentle old soul, and I realise May won't be riding him forever and that she'll probably progress to a larger pony soon, but Petra is very careful to make sure the pony matches the rider.' She paused, tilting her head to one side, her gaze intense. 'Why don't we go for a lesson?'

'What kind of lesson?'

'A riding lesson.'

'Are you serious?'

'Totally. We can have a private one, just me and you in the arena, and you can see for yourself what it's like.'

Jason wasn't sure about that. But he had been challenged, and he wasn't the sort of guy to back down from a challenge. 'You're on. When?'

'Before the gymkhana,' Rose said, 'and then you can make a final decision.'

'I've made a final decision.'

'Have you?'

He nodded, but for some reason he didn't think they were talking about gymkhanas anymore.

Rose couldn't believe Jason had agreed to a riding lesson. She felt like fist pumping the air but guessed it wouldn't be a good idea. She was under no illusion that he still might not agree to May taking part in the gymkhana, but at least she had done her best. She could tell that the little girl was absolutely desperate to take part, but Rose was conscious she might be interfering a little.

At least his suggestion had deflected Jason from her assumption that they would be going for another meal. Saying **I'll pay next time**, was just a figure of speech. If she'd been with one of her friends and had said the same thing, she would have thought nothing of it, but she wasn't with one of her friends, was she – she was out with Jason and she couldn't help it if she felt like she was on a date.

His mind was clearly on the upcoming riding lesson (she reminded herself to book it with Petra tomorrow) and he was asking what he should wear.

'What about a helmet?' he asked. 'Pamela bought May's. I don't own one.'

'Petra has got loads of spares,' Rose said. 'I'll have to borrow one of hers, too. And I don't have any jodhpurs either, before you ask. I'll just wear tracksuit bottoms; something stretchy is best, although jeans will do at a push. Make sure they're an old pair, though. But whatever you do, don't wear trainers. You need something with a heel and I'm not talking about a four-inch stiletto.' She glanced across at him to see that he was smiling.

'Why do I need a heel?'

Rose said, 'The last thing you want is for your whole foot to slip through a stirrup. A small heel, say half an inch, will prevent that from happening. If you've got an old pair of work boots, they would be ideal.'

'We're really doing this, aren't we?'

'You can back out if you want,' Rose said, 'but I'm still going to go anyway. It's years since I've been on a horse, and I don't know why I didn't think of riding again sooner.' Then she giggled. 'Oh, yes, I do; it's too darned expensive! Every now and again is doable, but once a week not so much.'

'When were you thinking of going?'

'I'll see when Petra can fit us in.'

'We could leave it a few weeks,' Jason suggested.

'Scaredy cat,' she teased.

'I'm not!'

'I think you are.'

'Okay, maybe I am, but have you seen the size of the beast Petra Kelly rides? Then there's the other one, Midnight I think his name is, the one Faith rides, or is it Charity...or perhaps it **is** Faith – one of the twins, anyway.'

'Don't worry, Petra will put you on an old plodder. And me too, I expect. There's no way she'd put you on something lively the very first time you got in the saddle.'

'Do you think there'll be one big enough to bear my weight?'

They pulled up in front of Rose's cottage but Jason made no move to switch the engine off, although he did twist around in his seat slightly to gaze at her.

Rose made a show of looking him up and down and tutting. 'I don't know,' she said. 'I'm not sure if there's a horse big enough for you,' and then she laughed when his mouth dropped open.

'Cheeky madam!' Jason exclaimed, also chuckling.

'I'll give you a ring tomorrow, shall I, when I know?'

'Okay, I'm looking forward to it.'

'Liar.'

His laugh was soft and did a funny thing to her insides. She shivered.

Jason made no move to kiss her, and as she got out of the car she was ever so slightly disappointed. She hadn't been kissed in a very long time, and she wondered what it would feel like to kiss Jason. She could smell his aftershave, and it was intoxicating.

Rose shut the car door, leaving him and his tantalising scent trapped inside.

He wound the window down and she ducked slightly to look at him.

'I enjoyed myself this evening,' he said.

'I did, too.' She took a breath. 'I meant it when I said I'll pick up the tab next time. If you want to go out with me again, that is.'

'Don't you want to see how rubbish I am on the back of a horse first? You might not want to be seen out with me.'

'I think I will,' she said. There wasn't so much of a hint of flirting in her voice, it was more like a promise.

They gazed at each other for a moment longer, something unspoken passing between them. Then Rose straightened up and began walking to her front door. She hesitated when she reached it and saw he was waiting for her to go inside. With a small wave and a sense of unfinished business, Rose unlocked the door and turned back to watch him drive away.

She hoped Petra would be able to fit them in for a riding lesson tomorrow, because she really wanted to see him again. And soon!

CHAPTER SIX

Jason hadn't expected the riding lesson to be quite so soon. He had no idea why, but for some reason he assumed Petra wouldn't have a slot free for at least a couple of weeks and certainly not until the gymkhana was over. How wrong could one be?

When Rose rang him this morning, he had still been in bed. Admittedly it was only just eight-thirty and he'd been awake for ages lying in bed and thinking, but he was nevertheless surprised to hear from her. When she'd told him their lesson was on for four o'clock that afternoon, he was even more surprised.

He was also slightly panicked. He barely had time to get his head around the notion that he was going riding, and there he was – about to go riding!

In a fit of nervous energy, he leapt out of bed and padded downstairs. He should make himself some breakfast, but his tummy was doing funny things, so he opted simply for coffee.

What was even more disconcerting, was that he didn't think the butterflies were entirely due to the riding lesson itself. He had a perturbing feeling it was because he'd be seeing Rose again.

He liked her a lot. Last night had been great fun and he'd seriously enjoyed spending time in her company. That he was also physically attracted to her was an added bonus.

But it also raised a warning flag – he was starting to get feelings for her, ones he wasn't sure he wanted. Since he'd split from Pamela, it had just been him and May, there had been no one else. Was he prepared for that to change?

Jason gave himself a mental shake. He was jumping the gun here, imagining all kinds, when they hadn't been out on a proper date yet. The meal last night was just food out with a friend. Today was just a riding lesson. Neither events could be described as a date.

Nevertheless, he spent rather longer than normal shaving, and he sprayed on his best aftershave rather than the everyday one he normally wore. He tried to choose his clothes with care but that was rather difficult considering the instructions had been to wear old stuff and work boots. It was only after he'd spent the greatest part of the morning faffing about with his appearance, that he realised what he was doing.

Gah, this was getting silly. He was behaving like a sixteen-year-old on his first date, when he was twenty years older than that and this wasn't a date at all. What the hell was he playing at? But even as he tried to distract himself by doing the laundry (crumbs, his life was so exciting) he still couldn't help thinking about Rose, wondering what she was doing now, and wondering if she was as nervous as he was.

And if she **was** nervous, was it because she would be getting on a horse for the first time in ages, or was it because she'd be seeing him?

Rose felt a little apprehensive, and she wasn't sure whether it was because she was going riding again, or whether it was because she was seeing Jason. A bit of both, she suspected. Then she tried to imagine it was her and Heidi going for a ride, and she realised she didn't feel quite as excited. Dammit, that meant the cause of her being so unsettled was Jason himself.

She shouldn't have suggested seeing him again. And she certainly shouldn't have suggested going riding. But she'd been thinking about May and her obvious disappointment at not been able to enter the gymkhana, and it had just slipped out.

It had nothing to do with wanting to see him on the back of a horse. Or see him again at all, for that matter.

Drat – she had to pull herself together. It wouldn't do to have these feelings for him, especially since he didn't appear to feel the same way about her. But then there was the look they'd shared, the long lingering one where she'd felt sure she'd seen something in his eyes which made her think she might be more than just a friend.

They'd agreed to meet at the stables, and Rose was the first to arrive. She saw two horses tied up outside the barn, then Petra came into view.

'Never thought you'd get that one on the back of a horse,' Petra said, jerking her head out over the rolling fields beyond the stables.

Rose turned to look and saw Jason's car trundling up Muddypuddle Lane. 'Neither did I,' she admitted.

'He must like you,' Petra said gruffly.

'Oh, I don't think so, it's not like that.'

'What **is** it like then, hmm?'

'Jason is just a friend.'

Petra gave her a scathing look. 'If that's what you want to believe, you carry on. But I've seen the way he looks at you, and if a friend looked at me like that I'd be bloody worried.'

Rose froze. If Petra had also sensed there was something between her and Jason, then maybe Rose's inkling about the look they'd shared last night hadn't been too far off the mark. But before she could explore the thought any further his car was pulling into the car park and he was getting out, and she caught her breath. Oh my god, he looked gorgeous. Suddenly she became aware of Petra studying her.

'Looks like you've got the hots for him, too,' Petra said, and Rose shot her an incredulous look.

'I haven't—' she began, then stopped abruptly, and Petra snorted in satisfaction.

'What goes on between you is your business,' Petra said, 'but my Uncle Amos gave me a piece of advice not so long ago. What he told me was, don't leave it too late. Think about it.' Then she turned away and began seeing to the horses and lengthening the stirrups, leaving Rose to mull over what she meant.

'Crumbs!' Jason exclaimed when he was finally in the saddle and looking at the ground. 'It's a long way down.' It made him quite nervous.

'Only if you fall off,' Petra pointed out dryly, and Rose sniggered.

Jason gave the pair of them a sour look.

'It's all right for you,' he said to Rose. 'You've been on one of these things before.'

He didn't even bother saying anything to Petra.

'Right, now you're safely in the saddle, I'm going to show you what to do with your legs, how to sit and how to hold the reins,' Petra told him. 'Rose, I can tell you've ridden before, so I want you to walk around the arena to let me assess your seat.'

Jason didn't like to say anything, but from where he was sitting Rose's seat looked just fine. He looked away when he noticed Petra scrutinising him and he felt a spot of warmth creep into his face. His daughter's riding instructor had just caught him ogling the behind of the mother of one of May's friends. Wonderful. Simply wonderful.

After a brief instruction from Petra, Jason's horse was told to walk on, and he nearly unbalanced when it stepped forward and he was forced to grab the pommel in a desperate attempt not to fall over backwards. To his surprise though, once he got into the rhythm of the gentle sway of the horse's movement, he found it was quite soothing. Gradually, throughout the course of the lesson, Petra had him turning left and right with total ease, and he was amazed at his control over the animal. He had a hint of how May must feel, so small, yet able to control something so large, just with her legs and her hands.

However, trotting was a completely different experience, and one he wasn't sure he was comfortable with. Especially the first few times, when he just slapped up and down on the saddle; he didn't think his undercarriage would ever be the same again.

But with Petra's patient instruction, it didn't take him long to get into the swing of things, and by the end of the lesson he had managed a rising trot, much to his surprise and satisfaction.

However, when he dismounted (far less elegantly than Rose) he had to grab onto the saddle to keep himself upright. His legs felt like quivering jellies, and he was certain he was walking like John Wayne. Jason thankfully unbuckled his helmet and handed it to Petra, who took both horses' reins and led the animals out of the arena.

'What did you think?' Rose asked.

'I enjoyed it,' he said, hearing the surprise in his voice. 'I think you might need to give me a minute though. I don't think I can put one foot in front of the other at the moment.'

Rose giggled. 'What you need is a hot bath, but I must warn you, you'll probably feel worse in the morning. Riding takes a bit of getting used to because you're using muscles you probably haven't used much in the past.'

Jason put his hands on the small of his back and leant first to one side and then the other. 'You can say that again,' he declared. 'I've never been so tense in all my life.' Then he sobered. 'I now know what May sees in it. It was quite exhilarating, and I didn't even manage anything faster than a trot.'

'If you never go riding again, at least you can say you've done it once,' Rose said. 'Did you feel safe up there?'

'Not at first, I didn't, but Petra is very good, isn't she? And so was Beauty. Although I felt she was only humouring me whenever I gave her an instruction. I think she knew what was expected of her.'

'She probably did,' Rose said. 'Petra's horses and ponies are very well trained, and she chooses them carefully for their temperament.'

'So you're telling me that I've got nothing to worry about when it comes to May going riding?'

'No, I'm not saying any such thing. You know as well as I that riding can be a dangerous sport, but then so can many others. Riding in an arena like this is probably as safe as it gets.'

'I should let her enter the gymkhana, shouldn't I?'

'It's up to you. You're her father, you're the one who has to make the decision.'

'But you're letting Heidi enter?'

'You know I am. Horses are the only thing Heidi has ever been interested in. I can't bring myself to not let her ride. It would be something akin to turning down her dimmer switch. Besides, I don't think she'd ever forgive me.'

'I don't think May is quite as committed.'

'She probably isn't, but she is getting a great deal of enjoyment out of it. As I said, it's your decision.'

Jason thought for a moment. 'You're right, it is. I think I **will** let her enter.'

Rose beamed. 'May will be absolutely thrilled.'

He stared at her, her face flushed, her hair slightly wild from wearing the hat, her eyes sparkling, and he knew he wanted to kiss her.

What the hell, he'd already agreed to two reckless things in less than twenty-four hours, he might as well make it three. So he took one small step towards her, bent his head, and kissed her.

For Rose the rest of the world completely disappeared when Jason's lips touched hers. For a split second she was totally taken aback, but the feel of his mouth, the scent of him, the way his arms slipped around her waist pulling her close, drove everything else from her mind until she was completely immersed in him.

She had no idea how long it was before he gently moved away, although his arms still encircled her, and she was filled with regret that the moment had to end.

Trembling slightly, she gazed up at him, those deep brown eyes drawing her in until nothing else, and no one else, existed.

'I've been wanting to do that for a while,' he admitted, his voice soft, his breath warm on her cheek.

'Me, too,' she told him, knowing deep inside how true it was. Stuff this friendship business; she didn't want just his friendship. It would be nice, but she wanted an awful lot more from him, and she sincerely hoped she was going to get it.

They grinned at each other, their noses almost touching, and she was about to go in for another kiss when there was a loud cough from behind.

They leapt apart and for a second Rose was mortified, until her happiness threatened to bubble up and explode.

'Sorry to interrupt your meeting,' Petra said, looking anywhere but at the pair of them. 'I was going to lock up for the day; I've got no more lessons you see, and...' She trailed off, clearly embarrassed.

'We were just about to leave,' Jason said, as Rose tried hard to stifle her giggles.

She felt like a schoolgirl being caught necking behind the bike sheds by the headmistress.

But as she stepped past Petra, the woman caught her eye and smiled.

'I told you he fancied the pants off you,' Petra whispered. 'Glad to see you took my advice.'

It was only when she was outside, Rose realised it wasn't her who had made the first move, it had been Jason, and she wondered what advice, if any, Petra might have given **him**.

It looked like he hadn't wanted to leave it too long, either, and the fact he was prepared to take a chance made her heart sing with joy.

'Where do we go from here?' Rose asked, later that afternoon. Heidi was still at her grandma's and Jason had invited her in for a coffee before she went to pick her daughter up. Rose hoped it didn't sound odd her asking such a forthright question, but she wanted them both to be clear on what was happening between them.

'The beach?'

'What? Now?' The evenings might be long drawn-out affairs, but she had to collect Heidi in an hour or so.

'I was thinking one day after school next week.'

Rose was dubious. Picklewick wasn't anywhere near the coast. It would take them a couple of hours to get there, and with school the next morning...

Her doubt must have shown on her face, because Jason uttered a chuckle. 'I'm going to bring the beach,' he said.

His statement didn't help soothe her misgivings. 'I'm sorry, I thought you said...?'

'I did.' He rose from his seat at the kitchen table and put his mug down. 'Come here.'

Rose got up and followed him into the garden.

'See that spot there?' he said.

'The one with nothing growing in it?' The garden sloped away from the house, and the lower third had been levelled and was empty of everything but soil.

'That's the one. I've recently cleared it because I was thinking of turning it into the seaside.'

'You've lost me.' Rose sighed with disappointment: he'd seemed so normal, too.

'May loves the beach – the sand, the sea, the little beach huts you get... I'm planning on giving her a taste of that in the garden. I've got some sand and pebbles being delivered tomorrow, along with some old railway sleepers. It'll take a few days for the guys I've hired to complete it, but once it's finished what do you say to helping May and me christen it? Heidi could put that swimming cap of hers to good use.'

'You're serious, aren't you?'

Jason shrugged. 'I've thought about this a lot. May has been helping me plan it, and she's chosen the pool and the summer house. I put my foot down at the donkey she wanted me to buy her, and the Punch and Judy booth she tried to persuade me to get. She also wanted a swimming pool with a wave machine, but we settled on one of those inflatable ones instead.'

'You **are** serious.' Rose was in awe. The theme of her own garden could only be described as neglected dead-swing turf. And the turf bit was debatable. There was something she and Heidi had that Jason and May didn't though, and after she'd fetched Heidi from her mum's she had a good root around in the attic until she found what she was searching for.

'Heidi? How do you fancy playing with papier mache?'

Jason was delighted with the way his garden was looking. It had been hard graft on his part and there were some finishing touches still left to do, but he'd booked a sneaky day off work and he'd managed to get most of it done.

Rose had offered to fetch May from school and bring her home, and May had been in a state of high excitement since the second she'd woken up, and she'd fretted that the beach hut hadn't been painted, and there wasn't any water in the pool yet, and a hundred and one other things. Thankfully, he hadn't let on he was taking a day off, otherwise he'd have had a devil of a job to get her to school this morning.

He had just enough time to have a quick shower and spruce himself up before Rose arrived with the children, but he couldn't help pausing for a moment to admire his handiwork. The pool was full and even though it wasn't particularly deep, he knew May would have hours of fun in it. He'd created a beach, and he was especially pleased with the pebbles and driftwood to the one side, with a boardwalk leading to both the pool and the beach hut. He'd painted the hut in pink, powder blue and cream, and he'd even had time to hang some bunting and fairy lights on the outside. Everything had been softened by the addition of the grasses he'd planted in any bare areas, and off to one side sat a table and a barbeque.

He'd fire it up shortly, but first he needed that shower he'd promised himself. To his surprise he was just as excited to see Rose again as he was to see May's expression, and it disconcerted him a little. Not since Pamela had a woman affected him this way, and he hoped he wasn't setting himself up for being hurt. He hadn't known how to respond when Rose had asked him where they went from here, which was why he'd blurted out the beach thing. He'd made it sound far more exotic and wonderful than he'd originally planned on it being (he'd had a paddling pool and a sandpit in mind, with the addition of a tonne of pebbles) but it had grown somewhat in the telling and he'd been forced to up his game.

He was pleased he had though, because the previously unloved bottom half of the garden now looked stunning. He'd been debating what to do with it for a while; May had consistently and repeatedly tried to persuade him it was big enough to keep a pony on, but he hoped she'd like this almost as much.

The doorbell ringing alerted him to Rose's arrival a short while later, and May barrelled in, flinging her little backpack and school jumper at him, as she raced

through the hall and into the kitchen, her
pigtails flying as she yelled for Heidi to
follow her.

Hastily Jason stood to the side to let
Heidi dash past, leaving him and Rose
alone for a second.

'Hi, you,' she said softly.

'Hi, yourself.' She looked delightful in a
pair of shorts and a strappy top, her hair
gathered up in a ponytail, and her skin
glowing.

Uncertainly, he took a step towards her at
exactly the same time she moved
towards him, and before he knew what
was happening he was kissing her
hungrily, his arms holding her tight
against his chest, his senses awash with
the scent of her hair and the taste of her
lips.

Girlish squeals of delight rapidly brought
him back to himself, and they broke apart

a second before the children stampeded back into the house.

'I love it! Thank you, Daddy. Rose, come and see. We're going to build sandcastles, and swim, and have hotdogs and burgers.' May was bouncing up and down.

Jason took the opportunity to leap in when his daughter paused for breath. 'You need to change out of your school uniform first, May.' He glanced at Rose, whose glow had intensified since he'd kissed her.

Rose held up a bag. 'I've brought a change of clothes for Heidi,' she said, passing the bag to her daughter, who thundered up the stairs after May. 'And we've got a present for May in the car, if you can help me with it.'

Wondering what it could be, he followed her outside and his eyes widened when he saw what was in the boot of her car. 'Is that what I think it is?'

'It's not strictly for Punch and Judy, and if you turn it around, you'll see that the other side is a kind of a market stall, but it's been in the attic for over a year, and I thought May could have it.'

Jason carefully slid the wooden puppet theatre out of the car and stood it up. 'It's even got stripey fabric around the bottom, like a real Punch and Judy booth. Did you do that?'

Rose nodded. 'And we made these.' She handed him a bag. Inside were Punch and Judy puppets and a crocodile cuddly toy. 'Heidi and I made the heads out of papier mache. They're a bit rustic, but I hope May will like them.'

Jason was speechless. 'I can't believe you've gone to all this trouble. Thank you so much.'

'May can keep the stand; Heidi hardly played with it. She was more interested in the model stable and horses she was given the same year. It's a pity for the stand not to be used, and if it gives May some pleasure...'

'Are you sure?' When she said the word "pleasure" his stomach fluttered and a thrill shot through him. He badly wanted to kiss her again. That this kind, wonderful, sexy woman wanted to kiss him back was electrifying.

Aware he needed to take things slowly (they both did), he gave her a hug and a peck on the cheek. He had to be mindful that there were other hearts and emotions involved than just his and Rose's, and no matter how much he was falling for her, or how invested he was becoming in having a relationship with her, he couldn't forge ahead without thinking things through. But later, when he saw her sitting on the sand playing with the girls as he took charge of the food, he couldn't help but think how right the scene looked. May had taken to her already, and the children got on extremely well together.

He just hoped he wasn't making a mistake by opening his heart to her. If she broke it, that would be awful enough; but if his daughter's was broken along the way, he didn't think he'd be able to live with himself.

CHAPTER SEVEN

What a wonderful day, Rose thought, as she drove along Muddypuddle Lane with a bouncing Heidi in the passenger seat. It was a glorious summer morning, the sky was an azure blue with not a cloud in it, and the day was already promising to be a warm one.

She got out of the car, Heidi bounding out ahead of her, the child hardly able to contain her excitement, and took a deep breath of fresh country air. There was a vague smell of horses, but the overriding scent was that of the meadow on the other side of the car park which was filled to bursting with wildflowers. A chicken scratched in the grass near the fence, making soft clucking noises to itself, followed closely by the cockerel, Frederick, who was strutting about as if he owned the place which, to be fair to him, he probably did.

The cat, Tiddles, was basking in the sun surrounded by her kittens, who now had their eyes open and were able to toddle about. Their mewling cries carried on the breeze, and she could also hear the sound of a goat bleating.

The gymkhana was being held outside and, as she'd drove up the lane, Rose had noticed various cones and poles all neatly arranged in one of the fields. When she walked across the yard, several horses' heads poked over the tops of their stalls and she could see they were already tacked up. She wasn't quite the first to arrive; she was close to it though, because she'd had immense difficulty in containing Heidi's excitement and the child had been itching to get to the stables.

But within a few minutes of them arriving the compound had filled up and the squeals of excited children rang in the air.

The horses and ponies could also sense the excitement and they tossed their heads and whickered to each other in their eagerness to be released from their stables. Petra had managed to transport the stage seating from the arena, and it had been erected in the field, along with a barrier to contain the spectators. There was also a refreshment van in the form of an old caravan which someone had converted, and she could smell the enticing aroma of coffee, doughnuts and frying onions, and she knew what she was having for lunch.

Automatically her eyes scanned the adults, looking for Jason.

It was less than a week since they had shared their first kiss, but they'd achieved several more since then, most noticeably the evening of the beach barbeque as she'd come to refer to it in her head, although finding opportunities for sneaky kisses hadn't been easy with the two girls around. Neither child had commented on it, but Rose was sure Heidi suspected something.

Rose didn't care. She'd made a promise after she and Ben had split not to be one of those women who introduced her child to lots of uncles, and this was the first time she had entertained the idea of any man being a part of her and her daughter's life. It was early days yet, very early, but she felt good about this. Every time she thought of Jason her heart fluttered and her tummy turned over.

There he was! She waved, rather too enthusiastically she realised, as a couple of the mums from school saw and nudged each other.

What the hell? She wasn't ashamed of the way she felt, and apart from being discreet around Heidi, she didn't see why she should hide it. They were both single and both consenting adults. It was nobody else's business, and if some of the other parents wanted to gossip, then so be it.

Jason made his way over and, to her delight and in full view of everyone, he gave her a quick kiss on the lips. It looked like he wasn't ashamed either.

'Fancy a coffee?' she asked. 'It should be starting soon, so if you find a seat I'll go and fetch us a couple of drinks.'

As she walked over to the refreshment van, she couldn't help thinking that to anyone who didn't know them they appeared to be a couple, and a feeling of contentment stole over her. She was happier than she had been in ages, and it was such a lovely uplifting feeling that she smiled widely as her heart filled with elation.

Jason leapt to his feet, cheering wildly and shouting, 'Go, May, go!' as his little girl re-enacted the scene from the other Thursday when she'd ridden her pony between a series of upright poles with little flags on the top. She was racing against another child, and she was going to win. Whoever won this heat automatically went through to the next one, and he was practically hopping up and down at the thought of her winning.

'Yay, well done, May!' he yelled, then turned to Rose. 'Did you see that, did you? She won, she's through to the next round.'

'Well done, May,' Rose called, then turned to Jason. 'You must be so proud of her.'

Jason nodded vigorously. 'I am, I most certainly am. She rode that pony like a pro.' He beamed, and saw that Rose was just as pleased for May as she would have been if it had been Heidi. The knowledge made his heart sing.

He watched his daughter as she walked the pony over to the holding-area and dismounted. Two more children were to go next, and the winner of that round would compete with May in the semi-finals. He gave his daughter a wave and her face wreathed in smiles.

'I won, Daddy,' she mouthed at him, and he gave her a double thumbs up.

He wouldn't have believed watching a few children dash up and down a field on ponies would be so much fun, but he was having the time of his life. Not only were some of the antics hilarious, like the egg and spoon race for instance (which he had no idea could be done on horseback) but there was also the more serious and competitive show jumping.

His heart had been in his mouth, as he watched the older children and some adults competing in the show jumping arena, and he'd almost lifted out of his seat every time a horse took a jump. He could feel Rose shaking with laughter next to him, but he didn't care.

The most exciting part for him, though, was when May was competing. It was all a bit of fun, but he was taking it almost as seriously as if she was in The Horse of the Year Show.

He sat back down and drew in a breath. 'That was tense,' he said, and Rose shook her head at him.

'You really are competitive, aren't you?' she joked. 'And to think you weren't going to let her enter.'

Jason was about to agree with her, when a shout went up. His eyes automatically searched for May. She was exactly where he'd seen her a few moments ago, in the holding pen awaiting her next go.

Relieved to see she was okay, he looked for the source of the commotion. One of the girls, he couldn't remember her name but he thought it might be Jane's daughter, was practising leaping into the saddle and jumping off again in preparation for one of the other games, and it looked like she'd missed and had slid off to land on the ground in a squealing heap.

The girl's pony, alarmed at all the commotion, suddenly swung his back end around, catching May and knocking her off her feet.

Tango danced out of her way, straight into the other animal's hindquarters. The creature bucked, his back hooves lashing out, and caught Tango a glancing blow. Tango, to Jason's horror, shied in response.

One of his hooves came down on May as he landed, and her scream of pain filled the air.

Jason was out of his seat in a heartbeat. Oh my god, oh my god, was the only thing he could think. Please don't let her be hurt. **Please!**

'I'm coming, May, I'm coming!' he called, running headlong, oblivious to anyone or anything in his way. He reached her at the same time as Petra, and he had dropped to his knees by her side and was cradling her head before Petra had a chance to check her over. May was crying and holding her arm.

'Are you okay, May? Speak to me! Where does it hurt?' he yelled.

Petra pushed him away. 'Let me see, and can someone please grab that horse?'

Reluctantly he moved to the side. Please let her be okay, he prayed, his heart pounding, his mouth dry. But when Petra touched May's arm and his daughter shrieked, he knew without being told that it was probably broken.

He looked up when he heard Rose say, 'Should I call an ambulance?' and anger surged through him. He knew he shouldn't have allowed May to take part, he **knew** it; yet he'd allowed himself to be swayed by a riding lesson and a pretty face.

But Rose's expression when he said frostily, 'No, thank you, I'll take her to the hospital myself in my car,' was something he knew he wouldn't forget in a hurry.

'Will May be all right, do you think?' Rose asked worriedly, and Petra shrugged.

'Of course she will. It didn't look too bad a break. In fact, her arm mightn't be broken at all, but it's better to be safe than sorry.'

Rose had just watched Jason carefully pick his daughter up and stalk off, the crowd parting like the Dead Sea to allow him through. She'd wanted to run after him, knowing he needed all the help he could get, but from the expression on his face the last person Jason wanted to see right now was her.

Why, oh why, did it have to happen to May? Just when Rose thought he was coming to accept his daughter's love of riding, the little girl had an accident. It could have happened to any of the children. But it had to be her. Poor little thing; she'd sounded as though she was in a great deal of pain, and Rose prayed she'd be okay.

Alongside his concern about his daughter, was the way Jason had looked at Rose when he'd rejected her suggestion of ringing for an ambulance – he'd looked as though he hated her.

And Rose had a horrible suspicion he blamed her for May's accident.

CHAPTER EIGHT

'May has had an accident.' Jason's voice was clipped as he spoke to his ex-wife on the phone. 'She's most likely broken her arm – it's not serious, but it could have been. And guess how she did it?' He didn't give Pamela a chance to respond. '**Riding**,' he spat.

'I'll be there soon as I can,' Pamela said, and he heard the worry in her voice, but that didn't make it any better. His daughter was hurt, and as far as he was concerned it was Pamela's fault for letting her go riding in the first place.

It was also Rose's, for being so blasé about it, and encouraging him to allow May to take part in the gymkhana.

But most of all, it was his own fault. Jason blamed himself for his daughter being injured. He should have put his foot down. He knew how dangerous horse riding could be, but he'd let it go. Actually, he'd done more than let it go; by allowing her to take part in the gymkhana, he'd actively encouraged it.

How could he have been so reckless?

Now he was in A & E with his little girl, who had most probably broken her arm.

He just hoped the break wasn't too bad and that it could be easily fixed with a cast, because if it was anything more serious he didn't know how he'd ever live with himself.

'How is May, Mum?' Heidi asked when the gymkhana ended, clutching her rosette.

Rose took it from her absently and popped it into her bag. Heidi had won an event but Rose wasn't sure which one, because she'd been too busy worrying about May and Jason. The distance in his face lingered in her mind, chilling her heart and freezing her thoughts.

'I don't know, sweetie. He hasn't replied to my text.' Or her phone call. She hoped it was because he had no signal, or no charge, and not because May was being rushed into surgery, or something equally awful.

Of course, he could be ignoring her, and deep down she didn't blame him. If she hadn't taken him riding, if she hadn't encouraged him to let May enter the gymkhana, his daughter wouldn't be in this position.

'I'm worried about her,' Heidi said. 'Do you think she'll be all right?'

'I'm sure she will be. People break arms all the time. She'll probably have to have a cast on for about six weeks, and have to do some exercises afterwards to help strengthen it, but in no time at all she'll be back to normal.' Unless she had to have surgery and metal pins and—

Rose pushed the thought away. She needed to think positively. May was going to be all right, she had to be.

'Rose?' a voice called, and Rose turned to see Petra hurrying towards her. 'Any news?'

'Nothing yet.' Rose pulled a face. 'I'm sure Jason will be in touch when he knows something.'

'It's not your fault,' Petra said astutely. 'You can't go blaming yourself. Accidents happen.'

'Yes, but if I hadn't—'

'He's a grown man. He made the decision to let May have riding lessons.'

'But that's the thing – I think he was railroaded into it by his ex-wife.' Rose glanced around, wondering how much she should say in front of Heidi, but Heidi had moved off a little and was chatting to one of the other girls. 'Jason didn't want May to have riding lessons in the first place, and he seriously hadn't wanted her to enter the gymkhana. I persuaded him to let her.'

'He could still have said no,' Petra pointed out, 'but I see where you're coming from. You can't blame yourself. No one is to blame. As I said, accidents happen. She could just have easily have fallen off the slide in the park, or tripped over the pavement.' Petra's eyes bored into her as Rose wrung her hands.

'Do you think he has a point?' she asked. 'Should I pay more attention to Heidi's safety?'

Petra shrugged. 'It's up to you, of course. Life isn't without risk, and forbidding Heidi from riding will negate some of that risk, but how unhappy will it make her?'

'Mum! You can't!'

Rose looked around to see Heidi's stricken face, and her heart dropped to her boots. Great, her daughter had overheard the conversation and now she'd have to deal with the fallout.

'You can't stop me riding. You wouldn't be so mean!' Heidi's eyes filled with tears. 'It's the only thing I've ever wanted to do, and you're going to stop me doing it. I hate you!' She whirled around and ran off.

Rose wasn't sure what she should do. The thought of Heidi with a broken arm made her blood go cold. The thought of Heidi with a worse injury absolutely terrified her. Yet riding and being around horses was the only thing her daughter was passionate about. Could she honestly take that away from her? And if she did, would her daughter ever forgive her?

She guessed she'd already lost the man she loved – was she prepared to lose her daughter too?

The ringing of his doorbell jerked Jason out of his thoughts, and he glanced at the time. It was gone eight o'clock, and he guessed it was probably Pamela. He'd expected her hours ago.

'Where the hell have you been?' he demanded.

'I was away for the weekend; you knew that. How is she?'

He opened the door wider to let his ex-wife in. 'She's in bed, asleep. I would appreciate it if you didn't wake her.'

Pamela glared at him. 'I wouldn't dream of waking her. But she's my daughter too, and I want to see for myself that she's okay. Where's the break?'

Jason rubbed a hand over his face. 'It's not a break, it's a sprain. No thanks to you.'

'What the hell is that supposed to mean?'

He kept his voice as low as Pamela's, so as not to wake May, but he felt like shouting.

'Do you know how dangerous riding is?' he growled.

Pamela sighed and rolled her eyes. 'Not this again.'

'Don't you care that she could have been killed?'

'Aren't you exaggerating? I rang Petra at the stables, so I know what happened.

I'm going upstairs to see my daughter. When I come back down, we'll continue this conversation.'

Jason shook his head in despair. Pamela hadn't been there; she hadn't seen their daughter knocked off her feet and trampled on. She hadn't had to sit for hours in the hospital, waiting for a crying May to be examined by the doctor. She hadn't had to wait anxiously for the results of the X-ray, and she hadn't had to soothe May off to sleep.

She hadn't had to witness their daughter's pain.

There was something else he was glad Pamela hadn't witnessed and that was May begging to be allowed to go riding again. Just before his daughter had drifted off to sleep, she'd pleaded with him with fresh tears in her eyes. If Pamela had seen that, she would definitely have promised to allow May to continue riding.

That was never going to happen. Jason would do everything and anything to prevent his daughter from being hurt again.

Rose sighed and picked up the phone. She put it down, only to pick it up once more. She was desperate to hear how May was, but she'd sent Jason a couple of texts and had called him twice, and he hadn't responded. Why would she think this time would be any different?

She had to try though; she couldn't just let it lie. For one thing, she was genuinely concerned, and for another she just wanted to tell him how sorry she was that it had happened.

She was listening to the ringtone with half an ear, not expecting him to answer, so she nearly jumped out of her skin when he said, 'Hello?'

'Hi, Jason, it's...um...Rose.' He'd taken her by surprise, and she was stammering.

'I know.' He sounded very distant.

'How is May?'

'It's a bad sprain, not a break.'

Rose could almost hear him say **no thanks to you.** 'Thank goodness for that,' she said. 'How is she in herself?'

'Exhausted. In pain. What you'd expect really.'

'I'm just glad it wasn't anything worse,' Rose said.

'So am I.'

Rose thought she might as well take the bull by the horns. 'I don't expect she'll be going riding again,' she said.

'That's correct. The next time she'll go anywhere near a horse it will be over my dead body.'

Rose heard someone mutter in the background, 'If that's what it takes,' and she froze. The voice belonged to a woman, and she took an educated guess that it was Pamela.

'Well, good, I'm glad she's okay. Tell her Heidi was asking after her, won't you?' Rose said.

'Will do,' he replied, then ended the call without saying goodbye and Rose was left listening to a dead line.

That told her, she thought. At least she wouldn't have to see him again if May wasn't going riding. Heidi would be a little upset, but she'd get over it, she had plenty of other friends and she could still see May in school.

Rose, on the other hand, was incredibly unhappy to think she'd never see Jason again, apart from around the village occasionally. In the short time they'd been seeing each other, she'd managed to fall in love with him.

 More fool her. She should have known better. Jason Halligan had too much baggage, and she wasn't talking about his daughter. May was an absolute delight, and both Rose and Heidi enjoyed spending time with her, but she didn't think Jason was emotionally equipped to be in another relationship just yet, especially since childcare was split so equally between him and his ex-wife. Prior to this, Rose had had reservations about how any relationship with him could work, but when she'd taken things a step further and imagined the four of them living together (more than a step further, more like a giant leap) she couldn't imagine how things would work when May would be at her mum's for half the week, and Heidi would be there all the time.

It wouldn't work, would it? Resentment would bound to develop, despite their best efforts.

So, in a way, this was probably for the best, although she wished May hadn't been hurt in the process. May, however, would recover soon enough.

Rose's recovery, on the other hand, would take a little longer, because she had fallen head over heels for Jason Halligan and her heart was sorely broken.

'Was that Petra?' Pamela asked as Jason ended the call.

'No. I've already texted her to say May is okay.'

Pamela folded her arms across her chest and leant against the door frame. 'If it wasn't Petra, I'm guessing it was Rose,' she said. 'May has told me all about her and Heidi.'

'I don't know what she's said, but there isn't anything to tell.' Jason knew he was getting defensive, but he didn't want to discuss Rose with Pamela right now. Or ever. He and Rose were over. But even as he thought it, there was an awful ache in his heart, and his stomach twisted.

He grunted in annoyance. Yes, he felt something for her, but he'd get over it. Time and distance always worked. He just had to make himself believe that.

'I hope you didn't wake May,' Jason said.

'No, I didn't, she was still awake.'

'She was fast asleep fifteen minutes ago,' he pointed out.

'Actually, she wasn't. She was just pretending to be because she wanted you to leave her alone.'

'Why on earth would she want me to do that?'

'Because she doesn't like you very much at the moment.'

'She told you that, did she?'

'As a matter of fact, she did.'

'I'm her father, I don't care if she doesn't like me.' Even as he said it, he knew it wasn't true. He wanted his daughter to like him, but sometimes he understood that it simply wasn't possible when you were a parent and you had to make tough choices and difficult decisions. 'My job is to keep her safe, not to be her friend,' he said.

Pamela narrowed her eyes at him. Their split might have been amicable but that didn't mean to say they hadn't had their moments of carping and scoring points off each other. He'd thought they'd moved past all that, but this riding business brought it all to the forefront again.

'Are you accusing me of not keeping our daughter safe?' Pamela's eyes narrowed and she folded her arms across her chest.

'You're not.'

'She's sprained her arm, Jason. She could have done something similar ice skating or in the playground at school, or climbing a tree.'

'For one thing, she doesn't go ice skating and for another, she doesn't climb trees.'

Pamela tilted her head to one side. 'She went ice skating for a friend's birthday, and yes she does climb trees. Admittedly, they're not very tall ones, but we have trees in our garden, and I've seen her on the lower branches a few times.'

'Why didn't you stop her?' he demanded.

'Because she's a child, and children have to explore. Didn't you climb trees when you were a child?'

Jason huffed. 'That was different.'

'How so? Because you're a boy?'

'That's not it at all. It's because I'm older now and I can see the dangers.'

'That's the problem,' Pamela said. 'You're not prepared to take a chance on anything.'

'If you're talking about our daughter's safety then, no, I'm not.'

'Actually, I was talking about you.'

Jason blinked. 'Excuse me?'

'May has told me all about Rose.'

'May doesn't know what she's talking about.' Suddenly Jason was aware of a little face peeping around the door behind her mum. 'May, what's up?'

'I **do** know what I'm talking about, Daddy,' May said with a sob. Her tear-stained face was stricken.

'Oh, poppet, have you been crying? Does your arm hurt?' Jason closed the distance between them, but May backed away, shaking her head.

Jason glared at his ex-wife. 'Is this anything to do with you?' he asked. 'What did you say to her?'

'Nothing controversial, and nothing you wouldn't approve of. Don't bring me into this. This is between you and May. And Rose.'

'Leave Rose out of it,' he commanded.

'Try telling that to our daughter. She thinks Rose is very much in it.'

'Please don't shout at Mummy,' May cried. 'Mummy stop being mean to Daddy. I hate it. I hate it, hate it, hate it!'

Pamela knelt down so she was at eye level with May, and held out her arms. May rushed into them, and buried her face in her Mum's neck, sobbing loudly.

Jason was mortified. 'I'm sorry, poppet. I didn't mean to shout at Mummy. It's just I worry about you; you know I do.'

May sniffed loudly and looked at him from under her lashes, wiping the back of her hand across her nose.

 Jason automatically reached into his pocket for a tissue and handed it to her.

'I worry about you too, Daddy,' May said.

Jason's eyes widened. 'Why are you worried about **me**?'

'Because you don't have anyone. Mummy has Craig, but you only have me. Rose only has Heidi.'

Jason gazed at Pamela. 'Is she matchmaking?' he asked, incredulously.

Pamela smiled up at him. 'I think she might be.'

'Well, I never. May, I like Rose a lot. But not in the way that Mummy likes Craig.'

'Mummy loves Craig, and you love Rose.'

'I think I'd know if I love Rose,' Jason pointed out.

'You look at her the way Craig looks at Mummy. Craig loves Mummy, so that means you must love Rose.'

Jason didn't know what to say to that, other than to protest.

But before he could gather his wits together and come up with something that sounded plausible, May carried on.

'You're cross with Rose because I got hurt riding, but it wasn't Rose's fault.'

'I still don't like the idea of you being on the back of a pony,' he said as gently as he could. It was breaking his heart to see her so upset about not being able to go riding anymore, but he sincerely believed it was for the best.

'I won't ask to go again,' May vowed, 'if you make friends with Mummy and Rose.'

Pamela shook her head. 'If you've fallen out with Rose over the gymkhana, then you're an idiot. You've got a chance to make a new life with someone, why mess it up?'

He was about to tell her it was because Rose had talked him into allowing May to enter the gymkhana, when he realised how pathetic it sounded. He'd made the decision; **him**, not Rose. He'd already accepted he was to blame, so why was he trying to deflect it onto someone else? Especially someone he loved. There, he'd admitted it.

His ex-wife stood, then bent down and lifted May into her arms. 'Okay,' she said. 'You win. If you're so worried about May going riding, I won't take her. Let's not fall out over this. May, I'm sorry sweetie, but your dad and I think it's for the best if you don't go again.'

May's chin wobbled, and her eyes filled with fresh tears.

'Before I go, I want to say one thing,' Pamela continued. 'Rose sounds lovely. Isn't it about time you took a chance on love?'

'I'll think about it,' was all he was prepared to say.

He might have fallen in love with Rose, but it was just too complicated, particularly since he wasn't prepared to let May go riding and Heidi would continue to, which was going to cause conflict between the two girls going forward. It simply wouldn't be fair on May.

Not just that, May only lived with him for half the week. Heidi lived with Rose all the time. Would May feel resentment because Heidi saw more of Jason than she did? It was certainly something to be considered.

With an increasingly heavy heart, Jason made his decision. He and May were fine as they were, and he intended for them to stay that way. The least disruption to May the better because she'd already had enough of that in her short life.

But when Pamela came downstairs after tucking May back in and assuring him that this time their daughter really was asleep, she said something that turned his whole world upside down yet again.

'Jason, we need to talk,' she began.

CHAPTER NINE

Even though Rose hadn't expected Jason and May to be at the stables the following Thursday, she was disappointed nevertheless. Apart from that one phone call on Saturday evening, she hadn't tried to contact him again. There didn't seem any point. Both of them were aware the relationship had ended – not that it had been much of a relationship to begin with. They'd hardly declared their undying love for each other, and she'd been pretty certain Jason wouldn't allow May to go riding again now that she'd been knocked over, even if the little girl hadn't sprained her wrist.

Rose sat in her customary seat in the viewing area, and watched Petra put her clients through their paces. Every lesson began this way, with a reminder of how to control the ponies, legwork, footwork, posture and so on. Rose tuned out a little, so she was rather surprised when someone slipped into the seat next to her.

It was Jane. 'Petra told me May suffered a sprain, not a break. I bet her father was relieved.' The woman was at it again, fishing for information.

'He was. I think we all were, including Petra.'

'Do you think she'll come riding next week?' Jane asked. 'Fleur wants to say how sorry she is. She feels partly responsible because it was her pony that made Tango shy.'

'I doubt it,' Rose said.

'Won't it all be better by then?'

'I doubt it,' Rose repeated.

'It must have been some serious sprain,' Jane said, and Rose realised she'd been talking about May's arm, not about her and Jason's relationship.

'It's not that. Jason doesn't like May riding. He thinks it's too dangerous, so I doubt we'll be seeing them again.'

'That's a pity. Will you pass a message on to him? Will you tell him Fleur is sorry, and that we all miss May?'

Rose said she would, knowing she was telling a fib even as she said it. She wouldn't be seeing Jason anytime soon. Maybe she'd spot him at the school gates now and again, but that would be it. She didn't even know whether she'd go and talk to him. These past five days had been awful, and it was going to take her some considerable time to get over him. Perhaps it was for the best that May wouldn't be coming to the stables any more. That way Rose could avoid Jason and give her broken heart time to heal.

Blinking back unexpected tears, Rose sent Jane a vague smile, then concentrated on Heidi. It was just the two of them once more. They'd survived it once, they would survive it again.

Jason helped May out of the car, even though her wrist was more or less healed and she didn't need any help from him whatsoever. His daughter was beaming, full of suppressed excitement, but all Jason could think about was whether he was doing the right thing.

'Hello, May, how's your wrist? Petra told me you'd sprained it.' Faith was smiling down at May. 'We didn't expect to see you this week,' she added. 'Are you here to ride? Or just to watch?'

'Ride, please,' May said. 'My wrist is all better.' She waved it in the air. 'See?'

Faith said, 'I'll go and fetch Tango for you. The lesson has already started – you've missed about half of it.'

Jason would have been happier if May had missed all of it. He'd still been uncertain whether to bring her or not, but she had been so terribly sad that he'd finally given in. He and his daughter had reached a compromise: May could continue to have riding lessons, but not enter any more gymkhanas.

May had agreed, but she had added a proviso of her own which had made Jason chuckle. She'd told him she would only go riding if he made friends with Rose again. He'd agreed willingly. Although their relationship had been of a short duration, he couldn't believe how much he missed her. And Pamela was right, he did need to start taking some chances. He intended to start with Rose.

The seat next to Rose was empty, and Jason walked over to it and sat down.

She didn't even glance up and his heart sank. She was ignoring him, and he totally deserved it. He'd treated her shabbily, and he supposed the first thing he needed to do was to apologise.

He leant closer and said quietly, 'I'm sorry.'

Then he jumped back in his chair as Rose let out a small squeak.

She turned a shocked face towards him and hissed, 'I thought you were Jane.'

'Nope, I'm Jason.'

'I can see that now,' she said in a normal voice. Then a slow smile spread across her face. 'You came. I take it you've brought May?'

'Her wrist is better. It's not entirely back to normal, but my daughter can be a very persuasive little madam when she wants to be.' He inhaled deeply. 'I owe you an apology.'

Before he could say anything further, Rose jumped in with, 'I should be the one apologising to you. I shouldn't have talked you into letting May enter the gymkhana, and I certainly shouldn't have taken you riding.'

'May isn't your responsibility. She's mine. I didn't have to go riding; you didn't make me. And you didn't force me to allow May to go to the gymkhana. That was all down to me. Those were my decisions, not yours. Please don't blame yourself.'

'Yes, but if I hadn't—'

'I can't wrap her in cotton wool, I realise that now. I think I might have been a bit over-protective. May and I have come to an agreement – she can continue to have lessons indoors once a week, as long as she doesn't take part in anything like a gymkhana. At least, not until she's a little older.'

Rose nodded slowly. 'That sounds sensible.'

'There's another reason why I decided to let her continue with her lessons,' he said.

'Oh?'

'It wouldn't be fair to May if Heidi keeps having lessons when she can't.'

Rose's eyes widened as she realised what he meant.

Jason continued, 'If we keep seeing each other, and I hope we do, May is going to make my life a misery if she can't go riding and Heidi can. Although, I understand if you don't want to see me again,' he added hastily.

'Why wouldn't I want to see you again?' Rose's voice was soft and a smile played about her mouth.

He stared at her lips, wishing he could gather her up and kiss her soundly. 'Because of the way I acted and...' He hesitated. 'There is something else.' Jason paused, wondering whether what he was about to say was going to make any difference to their blossoming relationship. It would certainly put them on a more equal footing.

'Go on,' she urged a bit too loudly and earning herself a shush from Petra in the arena.

Jason explained, 'It's about Pamela. She was away last weekend when May had her accident. When I phoned her it took her hours to return home. She and Craig were in Inverness. He's been offered a new job and he wants her to go with him.'

'To Inverness?'

Jason nodded.

'Will she take May with her?' Rose asked.

'No, she doesn't think it's right to take May away from all her friends and her school, and they'll probably only be there a year. Pamela is leaving May with me.'

'How does May feel about it? Is she okay?'

Jason's heart swelled with love for the woman sitting next to him. Her first reaction had been concern for May, and not about their relationship. And he knew that whatever happened, Rose Walker would put his daughter's interests before her own.

'She's a little upset,' he said, 'but I think coming to the stables has helped. We'll visit Pamela in Scotland as often as we can, and I assured May her mum would fly back once a month to see her. I know it's not the same as seeing Pamela several days a week, but this is the arrangement we came up with.'

'It can't be easy for Pamela, either,' Rose commented, and Jason put a hand on hers.

'I doubt if it is, but she said something to me that struck a chord. She told me you have to take chances in life. And that's what she's doing. It's what I want to do, too, if you let me. I want to take a chance on you, on **us**, because after all, life doesn't stand still and one day the girls will be grown and flown, just like the swallows in the barn when they fly south for the winter, and then it will just be you and me. If you'll have me.'

He hesitated, his eyes boring into hers, trying to gauge whether this was what she wanted. But she deserved to know the truth, so that's what he told her.

'I'm in love with you, Rose,' he said, 'and I'm taking a chance you feel the same way about me.'

Rose's heart was so full she thought it might burst. There was only one way she could respond – he was being honest with her, and she had to be honest with him.

'I'm in love with you, too,' she told him, and watched the worried expression disappear from his face, to be replaced by a wide grin.

'You are? You've just made me the happiest man in the world!' Jason exclaimed, and threw his arms around her. Before she could draw breath, his lips were on hers and he was kissing her so soundly that for a moment she forgot the rest of the world existed.

She was brought back to the present by the sound of whooping, cheering, and the stamping of feet, and they pulled apart to discover that everyone in the arena was smiling at them and clapping.

Even Petra looked pleased for them, and when she saw that Rose had noticed her, she gave her a big thumbs up. The only people who didn't seem to be amused were the ones having the riding lessons. Most of the children looked a little grossed out, and Heidi was pulling faces at her mother.

Rose didn't care. Jason was right; life **was** about taking chances and making hay while the sun shone – and this summer it was shining very brightly indeed.

The Stables on Muddypuddle Lane Series

Spring

Summer

Autumn

Winter

Valentine Kisses

The Patter of Tiny Feet

Wedding Bells

Christmas

About Etti

Etti Summers is the author of wonderfully romantic fiction with happy ever afters guaranteed.

She is also a wife, a mum, a pink gin enthusiast, a veggie grower and a keen reader.